John Mannock

The Poor Man's Controversy

John Mannock

The Poor Man's Controversy

ISBN/EAN: 9783744792196

Printed in Europe, USA, Canada, Australia, Japan

Cover: Foto ©Andreas Hilbeck / pixelio.de

More available books at **www.hansebooks.com**

Poor Man's Controversy.

By J. MANNOCK, O. S. B.

The Author of

The Poor Man's Catechifm.

A

POSTHUMOUS WORK,

Publifhed by his FRIENDS.

Be always ready to give an Account of your Faith.

PERMISSU SUPERIORUM.

T H E

P R E F A C E.

IN this fmall treatife, called the *Poor Man's Controverfy*, I have endeavoured to lay the matter open in the plaineft and loweft ftyle, that it may be underftood by the meaneft capacities, and have the better effect upon their underftandings and morals.

It contains, in fhort, the chief points controverted between Catholics and their adverfaries, and unfoldsall mifreprefentations and flanders of the doctrine and practice of the former ; fo. that in equity none can pretend to cavil any longer about them : for who are the beft Judges of our Faith but ourfelves, who know, believe, and profefs it, and expofe ourfelves to perfecution for it ? Is not the public more likely to learn it from ourfelves, than from thofe who are the moft ignorant of what we hold, or wilfully miftake our belief ?

It is an eafy thing to blacken others by affertions without proof : And very often prejudice: of education brings on great blindnefs in fearching out the truth of others tenets.

What I have wrote is without malice or ill-will ; wifhing my adverfaries the fame good as I do my own foul, *Truth* and *Virtue* : It is rather an apology for ourfelves, than an Invective againft them ; fo hope it may be taken in good part. I only wifh they would fpeak the truth in all they alledge againft us, which they certainly do not in their capital accufations, making us *Idolaters*, drowned in *damnable Errors* and *Superftition* ; by which they have figned not only our damnation, but that of all

A 2   their

their Catholic anceſtors, and the firſt founders and Apoſtles of the Engliſh Church, even Pope *Gregory the Great* and Saint *Auguſtin*, ſent by him, who by his preaching and miracles, converted the Saxon Inhabitants of this once bleſſed *Iſland* from Paganiſm. They ſhould not at leaſt any longer condemn our Creed of *Uncharitableneſs* in teaching, that out of the true Church there is no ſalvation.

Let them obſerve three words, and it muſt make a great converſion among them: *Veni, Vidi, Vici:* Let them firſt *Come,* and ſeriouſly examine our defence : Let them *See* the truth we hold, and upon what grounds : And this will *Overcome* Blindneſs, Ignorance, Prejudice, Malice, and conduct them to the truth which remains for ever. *The Truth of God remains for ever,* (Pſ. cxvi. 2.)

THE

Poor Man's Controversy.

CHAP. I.

On the Authority of the Holy Catholick
Church.

*If he will not hear the Church let him be unto thee as
a Heathen Man and a Publican*, Matth. xviii. 17.

2. WHAT is the root and foundation of
our Juſtification ?

A. Faith.

2. What do you mean by Faith ?

A. I mean a firm belief of all that God has
taught and revealed for man's ſalvation.

2. What are the grounds for ſuch a Faith ?

A. No leſs than the authority of God : I believe the myſteries of Faith, purely becauſe God
has revealed them all.

2. How ſhall I know with certainty that God
has revealed them ?

A. By the authority and teſtimony of the Holy
Catholick Church, which he appointed to teach them.

2. Is not this truſting to a human authority ?

A. No : It is a divine authority eſtabliſhed by
Chriſt, and upheld by his divine power : As the
authority of the Apoſtles and the Church in their

A 3   time

time was not a human but divine authority, for the same reason.

Q. Can I with entire security believe the Catholick Church in all matters of Faith ?

A. Yes : It is an Article of the Apostles Creed : *I believe the Holy Catholick Church, the Communion of Saints :* How come you not to believe it ?

Q. The Church perhaps may err, and lead me into error; how then can I safely trust it in all Matters of Faith ?

A. Because I am assured by the promises of Christ, who is eternal Truth, that his Church shall never fail, but teach all truth to the end of the world.

INSTRUCTION. Divine *Faith* is a firm belief of all those truths which God has revealed for our salvation. *It is the Gift of God,* and it is rightly said by the Council of *Trent,* that *it is the Beginning and Foundation of Man's Salvation, and the Root of all Justification,* (Sess. 6. c. 8.) *without it it is impossible to please God,* as it is written by St. *Paul* to the *Hebrews,* (c. xi. v. 6.) without it none can be disciples of Christ, or Christians. You see then of how great Importance it is to hold the true Faith, and you cannot be negligent or indifferent in the search of it, without hazard to your salvation and injury to the christian religion.

Now, this Faith must come to us recommended by a divine authority; by which I mean, that the divine mysteries and divine truths we are to believe, must be taught by some authority which God has appointed to teach them, before they can be the objects of my Faith. *Christ* had this divine authority, as being *sent by the Father.* The Apostles had it as being sent by him : *As my Father sent me, so I send you,* (John xx. 21.) And the Pastors of the Catholick Church, which they planted, have it by lawful election and ordination as their successors.

cessors. As therefore those who heard the Apostles, and believed the doctrine of the Church in their times, believed upon a divine authority, and had divine Faith of what they believed; so now those who believe the divine mysteries of the Christian religion, upon the faith and testimony of the Catholick Church, they also believe upon a divine authority, and have a found Faith, a *divine Faith.*

But those who believe according to their own private interpretation of Scripture, or that of some particular *National Church,* to which they adhere in opposition to the *Universal Church*; or of some *Teacher of a Meeting,* or *private Congregation of Dissenters,* they believe not upon any authority that has a divine mission to teach, and their belief can be no more than *Persuasion,* or *Opinion,* (as themselves commonly term it, and rightly) but not a truly *Christian Faith,* not a *divine Faith.* This truth is clear, and cannot be disputed, that not only the Apostles who were the first pastors of the Church; but also those whom they ordained to succeed them, are divinely established for the teaching of the whole world the truth of the gospel, and accordingly succeed them with like power and authority, that so all nations and ages to the end of the world may be taught the doctrine of *Christ,* which is revealed for the salvation of all.

Now, the same who received authority from *Christ* to teach his gospel and doctrine, received withal authority to decide all disputes about the sense of it, and to distinguish truth from error; seeing that to teach the Faith, and to note the Heresies contrary to it, is one and the same act in the teacher. There is then only one safe and secure way of believing right, viz. That which God has appointed; first, to hear the *Apostles,* and after them the *Pastors* of the Church which they planted. By

this

this means the world became chriftian, and by this alone we are fecured from error.

But that this fubmiffion and obedience of the faithful to what the Church teaches might be rational, and they firm in their belief without doubting; and that all obftinacy againft the authority of the Church might be for ever without excufe; to this end, when the Apoftles were fent by Chrift to *teach all Nations,* and received their divine miffion from him, for themfelves and their fucceffors, he added this folemn promife: *And behold, I am with you at all times, to the end of the world,* (Matth. xxviii. 20.) Alfo, a little before his Paffion, he had already made them another promife of fending the Paraclete: *I will pray the Father, and he shall give you another Comforter, that he may abide with you for ever, the Spirit of Truth,* (Jo. xiv. 16.) *Howbeit, when he shall come who is the Spirit of Truth, he shall teach you all Truth,* (Jo. xvi. v. 13.)

It is confeffed by all Chriftians, that the Church in the times of the Apoftles was made *infallible* or *unerring,* by virtue of thefe promifes of Chrift; for furely his perpetual prefence and the perpetual affiftance of the Holy Ghoft, are infallible means to make it fo; and where the caufe is infallible, the effect muft needs follow. For the fame reafon it has been infallible in all times fince; for the Church was no temporary inftitution, made only for fome particular times or people; but began in the Apoftles, and continued in their fucceffors, to teach the gofpel to all nations and ages to the end of the world. As therefore, the authority which Chrift gave to his Apoftles to preach his gofpel and baptize, was continued to their fucceffors, fo alfo was his promife extended to them, to the Apoftles, and to the whole Apoftolical fucceffion. This is evident; for he promifes to be *with them, at all times, to the end of the world*;

and

and alfo, that the Holy Ghoft *fhall abide with them for ever,* and *teach them all truth;* which includes the Apoftolical fucceffion of Paftors, as well as the fucceffion of faithful people, the Holy Ghoft being promifed and fent to both; though to the Paftors in the firft place, *for teaching;* and to the people *for hearing and obeying;* that fo the body of the Paftors and the Church may be for ever unerring.

And now you may conceive, how men who are fallible by nature, may be fo far divinely affifted, as to teach the oracles of divine truth without erring. In this fenfe, *Mofes* and the *Prophets,* the *Apoftles,* and the *Church* in their times, are acknowledged to have been *infallible* even by our adverfaries: And in this fame fenfe we maintain the Apoftolick Catholick Church to have been ever unerring by virtue of the fame promifes : So that the infallibility of God's Church is wholly derived to it, as it was to the Apoftles, from a perpetual divine affiftance of Chrift and the Holy Ghoft, *the Spirit of truth,* ever directing and leading both Paftors and People who obey them into all truth: which is ratherthe infallibility of God than men; he having it by nature, they only partaking of it, inafmuch as they are, according to his promife, affifted and taught by him.

In confequence of this *divine authority* and *infallibility* of the Apoftles and the Church, her Paftors are truly intitled the *Minifters of Chrift,* and *Difpenfers of the Myfteries of God,* (1 Cor. iv. 1.) their whole knowledge of the truth being from God, as well as their power and authority to teach it, and their infallibility in delivering it to the reft of the world. Confequently again to this, it is written of the Paftors of the Church: *He that heareth you, heareth me,* (Luke x. 16.) And in another place, *He that knoweth God, heareth us: And he that is not of God, heareth not us. Hereby we know the Spirit*

of

of truth and the Spirit of error, (1 Jo. iv. 6.) All which is confequent to the infallibility promifed them : As is alfo that of the Apoftle commending the primitive Chriftians, for that they had received his doctrine, *as it truly is the word of God*, (1 Theff. ii. 13.)

Hence again thofe glorious Attributes given to the Church in Holy Writ : Of *Pillar and Ground of Truth*, (1 Tim. iii. 15.) Of *Glorious Church without Spot or Wrinkle*, (Ephef. v. 27.) Of *Spoufe of Chrift betrothed to God in Rightesufnefs, and for ever*, (Ofee. c. ii. 19.) which excludes all notion of her *errors* and *corruptions*. We conclude that the prefent Catholick Church can no more deceive us than the primitive Church which the Apoftles founded : the fame promifes being made to the Church at all times, of a divine affiftance : *Lo! I am with you at all itmes, to the end of the world*; and the fame authority given to the Paftors thereof at all times to teach and to be believed. This Church, then, cannot deceive us, feeing fhe wholly relies on the covenant God has made with her, and fo our Faith refts more on his infallibility than hers.

Thus the authority of the Apoftles and the Church being divine, and appointed by *Revelation* to teach all the world the myfteries and divine truths revealed by Chrift for our falvation; we not only may fafely rely, but are abfolutely commanded to hear and receive their doctrine, under pain of an eternal *Anathema* : *Go into the univerfal world*, and *preach the gofpel to every creature*; *he that fhall believe and be baptized, fhall be faved*; *but he that fhall not believe, fhall be condemned*, (Mark xvi. 16.) Where the Saviour of the world propofes *Heaven* as a reward of fubmiffion and Faith; and *Hell* as the punifhment of our difbelief of thofe he has fent to teach.

And

And although many in the times of the Apoftles' might pretend other ways of coming to the truth ; yet as there was then no other fafe way of coming to it, but to hear the Apoftles and the Church, founded with divine authority to teach all nations ; and as there was then no other way of becoming a member of Chrift's Church and one of his People, but by receiving the doctrine which that Church taught; in like manner, however many in our times may pretend to fearch out religion by other means, and go after various teachers, yet there is no more than one fafe way, that is, to hear and follow the doctrine of that *One Holy Catholick Church*, whofe Paftors derive their ordination and fucceffion from the Apoftles, together with their power and authority to teach and to be believed. *By this we know the Spirit of truth, and the Spirit of error,* (1 Jo. iv. 6.) As it was the diftinctive mark of a Heretick in thofe primitive times, not to hearken to the doctrine of the Apoftles and the Church ; fo in all times fince, it is a fure mark of Herefy not to hear the prefent Church.

Now, as all are to learn their faith from the Church, it is neceffary that all fhould become members of it, and therefore neceffary that this article fhould be inferted in the Apoftles Creed : *I believe the Holy Catholick Church.* To let the world know by this publick profeffion of Faith, the certain and only way of coming to the knowledge of truth, and direct them where to find it. Accordingly, we read in the *Acts* : *The Lord added daily to the fame fuch as fhould be faved,* (Acts ii. 47.) In effect, have we not received our whole Faith, and all the myfteries of religion, from this *Holy Catholick Church ?* Our belief of the *Trinity, Incarnation, Baptifm,* the holy *Eucharift,* and all the other articles of our holy religion, together with the Apoftles Creed,

Creed, and the Scriptures themfelves ; none where-
of could be believed with divine Faith, unlefs we
firft believe the divine unerring authority of the
Holy Catholick Church, which recommends them
as divine truths ; according to that memorable
faying of St. *Auguftin*: *I would not believe the gofpel, unlefs the authority of the Catholick Church did
move me thereunto,* (Cont. Ep. Fund. c. 5.)

Moreover, the Church of Chrift being eftablifhed
not for any particular nation or time, but to convert unbelievers, and inftruct all nations in the
truth of the gofpel ; and this being as effential at
one time as another, it cannot be queftioned, that
it is effential to fuch a Church never to fail, but to
continue for the inftruction of all people fo long
as there fhall be people to be inftructed : Hence its
divine founder declared, *That he would build it upon
a rock,* and *that the gates of Hell fhall not prevail
againft it,* (Matth. xvi. 18.)

To conclude this matter ; if the primitive Church
was thus divinely affifted, the Paftors thereof had a
right to be believed, and to require of the People
whom they inftructed, to receive their doctrine, as if
it really was the word of God : And the Paftors of
the Church have the fame right and authority in
all times. Nor can this be called a *tyranni-
zing over our judgments* ; but rather, if God
has provided for us fuch an unerring guide as
his Church, thofe who know how to confide in
God, may with great fecurity believe all it teaches ;
nay, it is the beft fecurity, and the greateft bleffing he could provide for his people ; for by this
means, all the members of this Church, though of
the meaneft capacity, are as fafe and firm in their
belief, and in the expofition of Scripture in all the
controverted points, and as well affured of the true
fenfe thereof, as thofe of the higheft capacity ; all
                                                    having

having the fame unerring guide to follow, and all, fo long as they follow it, partaking of its infallibility fo far as never to err in matters of Faith. The following fuch an authority, is not in truth *laying afide reafon*, as our adverfaries would infinuate ; but *an act of the moft perfect reafon* : 'Tis not expofing ourfelves to the hazard of being led into error ; but a fecurity againft error ; againft the errors of our own *private judgment* ; againft the errors which *private Congregations* and *national Churches* when diffenting from the *Univerfal,* are ever fubject to ; and againft the deceit of all impoftors.

EXHORTATION. Learn from hence, O Chriftian ! on what fure grounds your Faith ftands, and how happy you are in following the authority of the Holy Catholick Church, fupported by a divine power. O ! what confufion of Sects and Religions have followed the arrogant pride of thofe who have diffented from her ! As Chrift is *her Spoufe, and has betrothed her unto himfelf in righteoufnefs for ever,* who fhall make a divorce between them ? As he is the *good Shepherd,* and the Church *his Fold,* how can fhe go aftray ? (Jo. x. 11. 16.) As he is *Head over the whole Church,* (Ephef. i. 22.) *Head* of the Heads thereof, as well as People, how can thofe who have received from him a divine authority to govern her on earth, lead her into errors, while, at the fame time, according to his promife, *he is ever with them ?* Befeech God to open the eyes of thofe who are departed from her, that they may return again as loft fheep to this *one Fold of Chrift,* remembering his faying, *There fhall be one Fold, and one Paftor,* (Jo. x. 16.)

CHAP.

C H A P. II.

The Church of God the Pillar and Ground of Truth,
(1 Tim. iii. 15.)

Q. I AM not yet quite fatisfied about the Infallibility of the Church : What is meant by it ?

A. That fhe is not fubject to err in matters of
Faith.

Q. How can fhe be unerring while fhe is governed by men who are fallible ?

A. Although the Paftors who govern the Church
are fallible by nature, God furely can preferve them
and his Church from error.

Q. Cannot the Church err at leaft in points not
fundamental ?

A. No : There is no difference in this cafe
between one and the other, they being all equally revealed truths, and the Church having the fame divine authority to teach them all.

Q. Is the infallibility in her general Councils ?

A. Yes : The definitions of her general Councils in matters of Faith ought to be received as the
dictates of the Holy Ghoft: And every general
Council has the fame right to fay as the Council of
Jerufalem faid at the iffuing out of its Decree : *It hath
feemed meet to the Holy Ghoft, and to us.* (Acts xv. 28.)

INSTRUCTION. As Chrift eftablifhed
a Church on earth to teach the truth of his gofpel to the end of the world, fhe cannot fail, nor
confequently fall into errors againft that truth ;
for were fhe to teach fuch errors, fhe would ceafe
to be the Church of Chrift, and then he would have
no Church on earth either to convert unbelievers

or

or to preferve the faithful from herefy. If the Church
he founded fhould err, whom have we to confult in
matters of Faith when controverted ? If fhe may
err, what certainty have we for our belief of *the Divinity of Chrift* and the *Holy Ghoft*, the *Incarnation* and
other myfteries of the chriftian religion, difputed
by former Herefies, and decided by her Authority
and her general Councils ? It is in vain to fay you
receive the definitions of thofe general Councils,
becaufe you judge that they decided according to
Scripture, for if the Church be not infallible, and
your judgment is alfo fallible, how can you be certain that thofe Councils decided according to the
true fenfe of Scripture ?

Now, the infallibility of the Church is not
founded upon fallible men, but on God who is infallible. The affurance we have of the Church
ever teaching Truth, is the affurance of Chrift's
holy *Word* and *Promife.* The infallibility of the
Church is the infallibility of God's Spirit ever
protecting and directing ; firft the Apoftles, and
after them, their Succeffors, in preaching the truth of
the gofpel to all nations to the end of the world ;
which, as I noted above, is rather the infallibility
of God than men; and may eafily be underftood :
For it is in this fenfe, all confefs that Mofes, the
Prophets, the Apoftles, and the Church in their
time were infallible, in delivering the oracles of
truth to the reft of the world.

Now, as to *Fundamentals* and *Non-Fundamentals,*
there can be no diftinction admitted between them
as to our obligation of believing ; feeing God revealed one as well as the other, and gave authority
to his Church to teach them all as revealed truths ;
nor can we doubt of any of them, without calling in
queftion the veracity of God, which would be
Infidelity. Accordingly, no Council or Fathers ever
made any diftinction between them, as to our
obligation

obligation of believing ; but whatever point was determined by the Church as matter of Faith and revealed truth, was univerfally accepted by the Faithful, and remains to this day as fuch.

Upon the ground of Chrift's Word and promife, that he and his Holy Spirit will be with his Church at all times to the end of the world ; we believe, that all decifions in matters of Faith, iffued from general Councils againft herefy, are infallibly true, as being the dictates of the Holy Ghoft, and as fuch have ever been accepted by the faithful in, all paft ages. All general Councils may conclude with this divine faying, : *It hath feemed meet unto the Holy Ghoft, and to us.* So might fay the four firft general Councils, by whofe definitions former errors againft the *Trinity* and *Incarnation* were condemned ; which if not acknowledged infallible in expounding the Scriptures relating to thofe myfteries, what certainty have you at this day of thofe and other articles of your chriftianity, which have been difputed by paft herefies ?

Finally ; If the Church is fallible, how are you certain, that your bible is the pure word of God ? feeing you received it with the reft of your chriftianity from the Roman Catholick Church ; and if fhe is fallen into fo many *damnable* errors, how do you know this facred book, which came from her hands, has efcaped all her corruptions ? Without the Infallibility of the Church, you can have no *divine Faith* of Scripture, but only a mere probable human belief of it.

EXHORTATION. O ! Chriftian, what thanks are due to God for making you a Chriftian, a Catholick member of his Holy Church, and guiding you to all thofe truths, which will lead you to your final felicity by the unerring guide he has given you; whilft others following their own private fpirit are wandering from darknefs into darknefs.

Have

Have compaſſion for ſuch, and pray heartily for their converſion to the true Faith. See you live up to thoſe infallible truths which you are taught, leſt they riſe up in judgment to your future reprobation. *Believe not every Spirit,* as St. *Paul* admoniſhes; but only *the Spirit of truth,* which according to the word of Chriſt *abides with the Church for ever,* and *teaches it all truth.*

C H A P. III.

Scripture not the ſole Rule of Faith.

Underſtanding this in the firſt place, that every Prophecy of Scripture is not of private Interpretation, (2 Pet. i. 20.)

Q. IS not Scripture a ſufficient rule of Faith ?

A. No : It is not, without an authentick Interpreter.

Q. Where ſhall we find an authentick Interpreter ?

A. In the Paſtors that govern the Holy Catholick Church, the Apoſtles ſucceſſors, from whom we received the Scriptures themſelves.

Q. Can plain Scripture deceive any Man ? Is it not at leaſt a rule of Faith when it is plain ?

A. Doubtleſs it is ; but it is not always plain when it is pretended to be plain : And where it is plain, it is not always followed by thoſe who pretend it to make it their rule.

Q. Is not Scripture the pure word of God ? what need of any other guide ? Men may deceive us, but the word of God cannot.

A. The Scripture is the word of God ; but Hereticks do not follow it in the controverted points,

till

till they have, by their private Interpretation, made it their own word.

Q. Do not at least all Proteſtants profeſs to build their Faith on Scripture, and not on any thing elſe?

A. They do indeed all profeſs as much; but none of them in faſt build upon it.

INSTRUCTION. Of all deluſions there is none ſtronger than theirs, who fancy they follow inſpired writings, at the ſame time they follow their own, or their Hereſy's erroneous ſenſe of them.

We regard the Scriptures with the greateſt reſpeſt, as being the word of God, and own them to be a rule of our belief when rightly underſtood; but when interpreted in a wrong ſenſe, as they conſtantly are by Hereticks, their falſe Interpretation is not the word of God; to ſuch the Scripture is no rule of faith, nor judge of controverſies.

And whence, but from this very cauſe, from the Scriptures not rightly underſtood, (as St. *Auguſtin* remarks,) have ſprung all the hereſies in times paſt? Can then the Scripture be the rule of Faith to them who have made ſo many diviſions in Faith? Can the Scripture be the rule of Faith to every private perſon, while the true ſenſe and meaning of it is ſo uncertain to him? Not that there is any thing wanting of truth and authority on the Scripture's ſide, but much wanting on the part of men's vain conceits and imaginations, which have drawn many into grievous errors and fatal miſtakes.

But you'll ſay, when the Scripture is plain, then at leaſt it may be the rule of our Faith, and cannot deceive us. To which I anſwer, that *plain Scripture*, taken in the right ſenſe, cannot miſlead us; yet it is not always *plain*, when it is pretended to be *plain*. On the contrary, it is this appearance,

and

and pretended clearnefs of Scripture, that has filled the Chriftian world with endlefs difputes. Do not all the Sects in Chriftendom appeal to *plain Scripture*; even while they diffent from one another, and from the Catholick Church?

Which of the reformed Churches, or Proteftant Sects do not profefs, and perfuade themfelves that they have Scripture, *plain Scripture*, on their fide, in all their differences of religion? The *Lutherans* in *Germany*; the *Calvinifts* in *Geneva*; the *Zwinglians* in *Switzerland*; the *Socinians* in *Tranfilvania*; the *Proteftants* of the Church of *England*; the *Prefbyterians* in *Scotland*; the *Anabaptifts*; the *Independents*; all pretend to build their contradictory tenets upon Scripture: Yet Faith tells us as well as reafon, that thefe their differences and contradictory fyftems of opinion and doctrine, are not in the Scriptures: Then, where are they but in the miftaken underftandings of thofe who undertake to be their own Interpreters? Thus you fee the Scripture is not always *plain*, when it is pretended to be plain; and yet it cannot be a rule of Faith fo as to unite all Chriftians in the fame belief, till it is fo plain, in all controverted points, as to make all parties agree which is the plain fenfe of it; which will never be, fo long as men have different minds, and will follow them.

On the other hand, Scripture is not always followed by thofe who pretend to make it the rule of their Faith, even where it is the *plaineft:* St. *Auguftin* remarks, that the Scripture is no where fo plain, as for the divine authority of the Catholick Church; yet *Diffenters*, like the *Donatifts* in St. *Auguftin*'s time, rather chufe to defert the clearnefs of Scripture, than fubmit to that authority.

Nay, it may be eafily proved, that of all the *Sectaries* who pretend to build their Faith on Scripture,

ture, and on no other grounds, none of them in fact do build upon it ; for with a very little reflection they cannot but see, that they follow it no otherwise than as it is expounded to them : Some expounding it by their own *private Judgment*; others according as they see it interpreted by some *Teacher of a Meeting*, or *Private Congregation*, or their *National Clergy* : So that they do not in truth follow the pure word of God, but only that sense of it, which some of these Interpreters attribute to it ; who, by their contradictions to one another, have given full proof to the world, that they do not all expound it in the right sense : Then, their followers in that case are not guided by *the pure Word of God*, but by the authority of *mistaken men*, and upon this their religion is built. This is evident. I may add, that none of them in fact have learned their religion by reading Scripture, but by the Instruction of Parents, Ministers, and Catechisms, by which they are all taught the tenets of their Sect, and all chuse their religion, before they have ever read the Scriptures, or are in any capacity to understand them. So far is it from truth, that Protestants all build their Faith on Scripture, and on nothing but Scripture.

When therefore you take the written Word for your rule, let the Church be your Judge for the sense of it, and you will have nothing to fear. The Church is the only authentick Judge, what books are to be held as canonical Scripture ; what translation to be received, and what the true sense of the text in controverted points. By the Church here we mean the Pastors of the Church, with the supreme head the successor of St. *Peter*, whether in a general Council or out of it : These have received from Christ a divine authority to teach and to be believed : To teach, I say, the *written Word*,

as well as the *unwritten*, and conſequently to expound it when the ſenſe is diſputed : For to teach
the word of God, and expound the true ſenſe of it,
is one and the ſame act in the teacher, as I noted
above.

EXHORTATION. Is it not then, O
Chriſtian ! a ſafer way to be guided as God has
directed, than to follow guides which are not of his
appointment? Is it not ſafer to truſt to the doctrine
and judgment of that Church to which all the pro-
miſes were made, and to which was given the whole
authority to teach, than to follow *private Teachers*
in the Interpretation of Scripture, who are not ſe-
cured from error by any promiſe of God.

O my ſoul ! truſt not to ſuch, but only to thoſe
who have received from Chriſt the authority to
teach, and to be believed, the Apoſtles, I mean,
and their Succeſſors, the Paſtors of the Holy Catholick Church. 'Twas by hearing them the world
became chriſtian ; by hearing them the Orthodox
have ever been preſerved from all paſt hereſies :
To them he ſaid, *Behold I am with you at all times,
to the end of the world.* This he did not ſay to any
one particular *national* or *local Church, Meeting,* or
private Congregation, or the *Teachers* of them ; but
to the *Univerſal* or *Catholick Church* ever holding *One
Faith* and *Communion.* Follow theſe whom God
has appointed to be your guide ; otherwiſe, 'tis *the
blind leading the blind, till both fall* into the ditch.

CHAP.

C H A P. III.

On *Private Judgment,* and *Private Spirit.*

Every Prophecy of Scripture is not of private Interpretation, (2 Pet. i. 20.)

Q. WHAT do you mean by *private Judgment?*
A. To be guided by one's own fenfe, independently of all Church authority for the interpretation of Scripture.

Q. Why may not every one be allowed to follow the Scripture, according to the beft of his Judgment in matters of Faith?
A. It is a moft pernicious maxim ; it deftroys all obedience to the Church, which we are commanded to hear ; befides many other evils that have fprung from it.

Q. What are thofe evils?
A. Innumerable fects in Faith and Religion ; no Herefy but what took its beginning from it.

Q. At leaft why may not I be allowed to follow my *Teacher,* or the *Congregation,* or *National Church* I belong to?
A. No National Church, no private Congregation or Teacher, diffenting from the Univerfal or Catholick Church, can be a fafe guide to their followers : All Sectarifts and Hereticks follow fuch guides.

Q. Why may we not, at leaft, follow the *Inftinct of the Spirit* ; the Spirit of God cannot deceive me.
A. Very true ; the Spirit of God cannot deceive you, nor be deceived : But you may be deceived by thofe who make you believe, that you follow the Inftinct of the Spirit of God when you do not.

INSTRUCTION. *Private Judgment,* which makes a man his own Judge in controverted points

of

of Faith and religion, never was allowed of in the Church of God, but condemned by all antiquity. All controversies of Faith from the very beginning of the Church, were decided by the authority of the Church. The firſt controverſy about the neceſſity of *Circumciſion* for the converted Gentiles, was determined in a Council at *Jeruſalem*, not left to the private Judgment of the contending parties : And all the ſequent controverſies; as of the time for celebrating *Eaſter* ; of the *Trinity* of Perſons in God ; of the *Divinity* of *Chriſt*, and the *Holy Ghoſt* ; of the *Incarnation* ; of the *Power of the Church* to remit ſin to thoſe who fall after Baptiſm ; of *Grace*; of *Original Sin* ; all theſe controverſies were determined by Church authority againſt ancient Hereticks. *Luther* and *Calvin* own the condemnation of them to be juſt, and that thoſe who maintained them are to be accounted as Hereticks. But had private Judgment been the Judge, and all parties been allowed an equal right to expound Scripture for themſelves in thoſe controverted points. I apprehend thoſe diſputes had not been ended to this day : Nor can it be known with certainty, if the infallibility and authority of the Church be ſet aſide, whether the parties condemned, or thoſe who condemned them, had truth on their ſide. Private Judgment has raiſed many diſputes in religion, but never ended one.

The Scripture itſelf teaches, that the Scripture is not to be interpreted by private Judgment : As it is written in St. *Peter*, (Ep. 2. c. i. v. 20.) *Every Prophecy of Scripture is not of private Interpretation : for not by human will was Prophecy brought at any time ; but the Holy Men of God ſpoke, inſpired by the Holy Ghoſt.* Here the reaſon is given why the Scriptures are not to be expounded by every man's

privat

private Judgment ; becauſe every part of the holy Scripture was delivered by the Holy Ghoſt, by whom the ſacred writers were inſpired. By whom then are they to be interpreted when their ſenſe is diſputed, but by thoſe to whom the Holy Ghoſt was promiſed and ſent for *the teaching them all Truth ?* the Apoſtles and their Succeſſors the Paſtors of the Catholick Church : *Howbeit, when he, the Spirit of Truth, ſhall come, he will teach you all Truth,* (Jo. xvi. v. 13.) A promiſe not made to every particular perſon that undertakes to expound Scripture by his own *private Judgment.* Moreover :

As private Judgment deſtroys all obedience to the Church, it cannot ground a certain belief, becauſe every man's private Judgment is ſubject to error. Thoſe therefore who leave the divine unerring authority of the Church Catholick, to follow their own private Interpretations of Scripture, can have no divine Faith of what they believe ; becauſe, although the Scripture which they pretend to make the rule of their belief, be infallible truth, their Interpretation is not but liable to miſtake ; and thus their private Judgment being ever apt to embrace error as well as truth, when left to itſelf, whatever belief is built upon it, is no more than *Opinion,* not *Chriſtian Faith,* which excludes all deliberate doubt and uncertainty : So that this maxim of expounding Scripture by *private Judgment* deſtroys all certainty of the Chriſtian Faith, eſpecially in points controverted.

Some indeed among thoſe who diſſent from the Catholick Church, pretend they do not follow *their own private Judgment,* but the *national Church,* or their *Teachers,* not conſidering, that a national Church diſſenting from the Catholick or Univerſal Church, does but follow the private Judgment of its firſt Reformers : As do alſo private meetings and congregations;

gations ; and therefore theſe are no more ſufficient to ground divine Faith upon, than was the *private Judgment* of thoſe that founded them. Beſides, thoſe who firſt model their Faith by their own ſenſe of Scripture, (which is a right allowed to every one in all the reformed Churches,) and then approve of that Church which approves them, do not in effect believe their Church, but themſelves.

The ſame is to be ſaid of thoſe who believe by pretended *Inſtincts of the Spirit.* For though the teſtimony of the Holy Ghoſt be a ſufficient ground of divine Faith ; yet there being no ſure teſtimony produced to ſhew who are led by this divine Spirit, and no promiſe of God for it ; nor proof given, whereby we may clearly diſcern the motions of the *Holy Ghoſt* from other motions of *Fanaticiſm* ; there cannot be ſuch certainty in theſe pretended *Inſtincts of the Spirit*, as divine Faith requires; and the belief of thoſe who follow thoſe *private Inſtincts*, is not *Faith*, but only *Opinion*, or *Perſuaſion*, like theirs who follow their *private Judgment*, and no better. I may add, that the Sectaries of our times who p.etend to be led by the *Inſtincts of the Spirit*, are found to contradict one another moſt furiouſly, at the ſame time that all cry, *The Spirit of the Lord ! The Spirit of the Lord :* which plainly ſhews by what ſpirit they are led.

In a word, you would not truſt the *private Judgment* or *private Inſtinct* of another in an affair of this great concern, nor would another truſt to yours : You eaſily diſcover in others how unqualified is *private Judgment* and *private Spirit* to decide matters of controverſy, and how dangerous it is to truſt it ; and yet while you are ſo ſenſible of the weakneſs of it in another, you think yourſelf and your own Judgment an oracle. But is this being prudent ? is this being wiſe unto ſalvation ?

· B   EXHOR-

. EXHORTATION. Away then with your *private Spirit* and *private Judgment,* and give place to the *Spirit of God,* and Judgment of the Holy Catholick Church supported by him. What authority has God given you to interpret Scripture, or to decide any Controversy of Faith? Can you shew this authority by any sign or miracle?

Reflect well on the many evils that have sprung from *private Spirit* and *private Judgment*; what *Errors!* what *fatal Mistakes!* what *Blasphemies!* What a variety of *Sects* and *false Religions* contradicting one another and the Truth! True is the saying of a holy Father, (St. *Bernard*) *He that hath himself for his Master, hath a Fool for his Scholar.*

As self-will is the bane and destruction of all Virtue, so is the *private Spirit* and *private Judgment* the destruction of all Faith and Religion. By the one we forsake the will of God to follow our own : By the other we revolt from the Faith of his Church, making our own will and judgment the *Standard* of Faith, till we have no Faith nor Religion at all.

C H A P. V.

On our Choice of the True Church.

I believe the Holy Catholick Church.

Q. HOW shall we know with certainty which is the true Church that all are commanded to hear?

A. The true Church is that which we profess in the Creed : *The Holy Catholick Church :* This is the ancient church from which all sects departed.

Q. What

Q. What other are the marks of the true Church?

A. They are diſtinctly ſet down in the *Nicene Creed,* which does but more fully explain that of the Apoſtles: In this we profeſs *the Holy Catholick Church, the Communion of Saints:* In that, *One Holy Catholick Apoſtolical Church.*

Q. Are theſe marks of the true Church to be found in no other but the Roman Catholick?

A. No: no other can make good their claim to them.

INSTRUCTION. The true Church of Chriſt, being that which he founded, and the Apoſtles planted in all nations, is by conſequence the firſt and moſt ancient, from which all others broke off; and the moſt ancient is that which never did break off from any other more ancient than itſelf: This is evident.

Now, let all who have care of their ſalvation, take this matter into ſerious conſideration, and they will preſently behold one Church in Chriſtendom a- mongſt many that take that name, and only one, conſiſting in all times of many national and local churches, all holding communion with one another, and with the Biſhop of Rome, as ſucceſſor of Saint *Peter*; acknowledging his ſupreme juriſdiction in ſpirituals, and all concurring in one Faith and wor- ſhip; commonly known and diſtinguiſhed in the world, by the title of *Roman Catholick Church*; from whoſe communion all other ſects, whether modern or ancient, departed, leaving her communion, as they pretend, for her errors: by which at leaſt this truth is proved by the conſent of them all, that the Roman Catholick is the firſt and moſt ancient com- munion of Chriſtians.

Now, as to thoſe who believe that the Church at its firſt foundation, was made by him *infallible* or *unerring* in teaching the truth of the Goſpel, they

cannot

cannot harbour any doubt, but the Roman Catholick, and no other, is the true Church ; becaufe it is
the firft and the moft ancient ; and if that has never
erred, then all others which have left her doctrine
and communion, have erred, and are *Schifmatical*
and *Heretical* Congregations ; which ought not to
have fo much as the name of *Churches* ; nor do we
find that name fo much as once given to fuch
throughout the New Teftament.

And as to fuch as ftill perfift in their oppofition
to her infallibility, and pretend fhe might err,' and
has erred ; it is impoffible for them to produce any
evidence of her errors, feeing thofe who accufe her
of error, confefs, that their own Churches and
teachers are alfo *fallible*, and *may err.* Suppofe
then fome private teacher of a meeting, or minifter
of a parifh, or a national fynod, interprets the Scripture in the controverted points, in a fenfe contrary
to what the Catholick Church defines ; this does
not amount to any thing like evidence of that
Church's errors ; becaufe this truth will ftill recur
to our minds, that thofe who accufe her of error, are
themfelves *fallible* and *may err in the accufation.* Hence,
even in their own fyftem of the *fallibility* of the
former Church, it does not appear how they have
mended their condition in leaving her communion
to join with others, who by their own confeffion
are alfo fallible : nay, it is evident, that they
have changed for the worfe, in deferting the ancient
Catholick Church, to which all the promifes of *divine fupport* were made, to follow *fallible teachers*
who have no fuch promife : and as there is no evidence of the former Church's errors, fhe is ftill
in full poffeffion of her whole power and authority,
and ought to be believed.

But moreover, we fhall now make it appear, that
all the marks of the true Church belong to the Roman

man Catholick Church and to no other. Thefe marks are fet down by the primitive Fathers in the *Nicene Creed :* in which this Article is inferted, I believe *One*, *Holy*, *Catholick* and *Apoftolical Church* ; that hereby the true Church may be known in all times.

Firft : We may remark, that in the Roman Catholick Church, and no other, all the members, tho' divided as to nations, intereft and language, and fpread over Chriftendom, yet all concur in one Faith and worfhip, receive the fame facraments, hold the fame principles of religion, all acknowledge the Bifhop of *Rome*, as fucceffor of St. *Peter*, to be Head of the Church, and all obey one ecclefiaftical authority ; and thus are perfectly *One Fold*, (Jo. x. 16.) and *One Body*, (Ephef. iv. 4.) as the Church of Chrift muft effentially be.

Whereas fuch as are fallen from this Catholick Church, are eternally divided among themfelves, having as many different Confeffions of Faith, as they live under many temporal heads ; the private fpirit and private judgment which they and their ringleaders follow in expounding Scripture, being the very principle of divifion.

Secondly : It was anciently prophefied of the Church of Chrift, *that all nations fhall flow unto her*, (Ifai. xxii.) Her firft paftors with their fucceffors were fent *to teach all nations*, (Matth. xxviii. 19.) To *preach the Gofpel in the univerfal world to every creature*, (Mark xvi. 16.) To *preach penance and remiffion of fins to all nations*, (Luke xxiv. 47.) *And their found went forth into all the earth, and their words unto the ends of the earth*, (Pf. xviii. 5.) *And the ends of the earth have been converted unto our Lord*, (Pf. xxi. 22.) *And all the families of the Gentiles have adored in his fight : And the Redeemer is called the God of all the earth*, (Ifai. liv. 2, 3.) His Church con-

fifting,

fisting, as in heaven, so on earth, of *all nations, and tribes, and people, and tongues,* (Rev. vii. 9.) Now, it is visible that the Roman Catholick, and no other, is the Church from which all nations first received their Christianity ; and as this Church converted all nations, it did thereby become the Church of all nations ; the whole universal, or Catholick Church, and justly at present claims that title as her own ; and as in all ages past, so at this day, is commonly known and distinguished in the world by the name of *Catholick,* which no heretical or schismatical congregation could ever yet take from her, or obtain for themselves : By this mark, the true Church is as visible as the sun ; as it was in St. *Augustin's* time, writing against the *Donatists,* when he said, the very name of *Catholick* was enough *to bind him to that church.*

Thirdly : The Roman Catholick Church has ever been governed by a Clergy succeeding the Apostles by a lawful ordination and mission : But where is the sect that can shew a succession of their Clergy and mission from the Apostles, as we can a succession of the Bishops of *Rome* even from St. *Peter?* 'Tis impossible : Their pretended mission and authority to preach and administer sacraments can mount no higher than the first founders of their sects. None then but the Roman Catholick can with any propriety be called the *Apostolical Church.*

Fourthly : As none but the pastors of the Roman Catholick Church derive their mission and authority from the Apostles, who received them from Christ ; 'tis only in that communion the right and due administration of sacraments, with the true worship of God, and preaching of the faith and doctrine of Christ, can be : And as these are the means of all justifying and sanctifying grace ; we must conclude, that in this Church, and no other, that

grace

grace and fanctity will ever be found, and visibly appear. In effect, all the faints, the *Blessed Apostles, Martyrs, Confessors, the holy Fathers and Doctors, holy Monks* and *Eremits, the holy Virgins,* the Founders of religious orders with their numerous followers, despifers of the world, leaving all to follow Chrift, the Apostles that converted nations, workers of miracles, all lived and died in the communion of the Roman Catholick Church. This then is the *Holy Way* of which *Isaias* prophefied : *It shall be called the Holy Way,* (xxxv. 8.) Not the broad way that leads to perdition, *transferring the grace of God into wantonnefs, promising liberty,* (Jude 4.) but the *narrow way* that leads to life, preaching confeffion of fins, enjoining penance, mortification, felf-denial, and urging the obfervance not only of the commandments, but evangelical counfells. In a word, the efficacy and holinefs of the doctrine of this church has been made *visible* in the converfion of all the infidel nations, in the repentance of finners, in the holy works of the faints that have lived and died in her communion; in the fanctification of all orders and ranks, who are ever holy, and advance in fanctity, in proportion as they follow the leffons which fhe gives them : And if others are wicked that live in her communion, 'tis ever in proportion as they degenerate from her doctrine and difcipline.

All heretical churches are confcious of the weaknefs of their title to thefe marks of the true Church, and therefore in their writings never go about to prove theirs by thefe characters.

EXHORTATION. What thanks, O Chriftian! ought you to return to God for all the bleffings beftowed on you! particularly for your vocation to the true faith and church, whilft thoufands are out of it, and live and die in error ! Praife God for not only giving to fallible men fuch an infal-

lible

lible, guide as his Church, to lead them out of all
the errors of tbe world, and preſerve them in truth ;
but alſo for protecting that Church to this preſent
time, againſt all the enemies and impugners of her
faith.   No attacks of error, perſecution, or tempta-
tion, could ever move her. As God is *always with*
her, who can be againſt her ? Ever have this firm
perſuaſion, that nothing ſhall ever deſtroy the holy
Catholick Church : *The gates of hell ſhall not prevail*
againſt her.   Stand firm to her, and no impoſtor,
not even *Antichriſt* himſelf, will be able to ſeduce
you.

But be firm and true to her, not only by your
Faith, but by the practice of your Faith. Let your
virtue ſhine as a light, by which others may come
to glorify God in their converſion to the only true
Faith on earth. As you are by Grace and Faith a
member of the Catholick Church, which is ſo viſible and renowned over the whole world, and intitled to be one of God's elect, live in ſuch a manner as may make your election ſure. And as he
has commanded his Church to make her light *ſhine*
before a dark and infidel world, and not to lie hid
under a buſhel, (Matth. v. 15.) ſo let your con-
ſtancy in faith, as well as in every virtue, *ſhine* as
a light to your erring neighbours, that ſo you may
convey the ſame to thoſe who ſit in *darkneſs, error,*
hereſy, and *ſchiſm :* So *let your light ſhine before men,*
(v. 16.)

Praiſe God again in the wonderful *Unity* of his
Church, nothing but a divine power could effect
ſuch an Unity. As the Church is *holy,* ſee you do
not bring a reproach upon its ſanctity by your bad
life and manners, and make the *enemies of God*
blaſpheme.   As God is holy, and his Church holy,
and ſo many holy ſaints are ſet for your example,
be you alſo holy.   As her Faith is *Catholick,* be-

lieved

lieved throughout the world, fo let your belief be entire and orthodox in every the leaft point. As fhe is *Apoftolical*, founded by Chrift, and received her doctrine and authority from him by a lawful fucceffion of her paftors from the apoftles ; be true and fincere to her doctrine and difcipline, and never think of running after thofe teachers who have no miffion or authority derived from them. Thus may you live and die fecure in this *bleffed Ark*, out of which there is no falvation.

C H A P. VI.

Our Lord added (to the Church) from Day to Day fuch as fhould be faved, (Acts ii. 47.)

Q. IS it not againft charity to fay : *Out of the true Church there is no falvation ?*

A. No : It is the greateft charity to affirm it.

Q. Why fo ?

A. Becaufe it is admonifhing him who is in error to feek and follow the right way to falvation.

Q. Which is the right way to falvation ?

A. To believe and join communion with *One Holy Catholick Church, the communion of faints,* which you profefs in your Creed.

INSTRUCTION. If Catholicks, upon occa-fion, admonifh thofe of a different communion, when they hear them faying, *that people may be faved in all religions,* that without the true Faith, and out of the true Church there is no falvation; it is evident there is nothing of uncharitablenefs in what they fay of this matter ; feeing it proceeds not from ill-will, nor rafh judgment, but a full conviction that the Catholick Church is the true Church of Chrift, which we profefs in our Creed ; confequent-

ly, that all ſuch as do not join communion with
this Church, are under the wrath of God, and not
in that way which Chriſt appointed for the whole
world as the way of ſalvation. In this ſenſe to affirm,
that out of the true Church there is no ſalvation
for ſuch hereticks and ſchiſmaticks, as through their
own fault and perverſeneſs are out of it, and live
and die obſtinate in hereſy and ſchiſm (admitting
at the ſame time the plea of invincible ignorance)
is, I ſay, not uncharitableneſs, but rather the greateſt
charity, as adviſing people to their eternal good, and
admoniſhing them to quit error, and to ſet themſelves
in the right way to heaven : this ſhould rather be
termed *Zeal* than want of *Charity :* It is the ſame
kind of zeal as moved the *Prophets* in ancient days
to call loudly upon the *Jews* to forſake their evil
ways ; much the ſame zeal as moved the *Apoſtles* to
expoſe their lives to propagate the truth of the
Goſpel. It is written in Scripture, *without Faith
it is impoſſible to pleaſe God,* (Heb. xi. 6.) If I endeavour to bring my neighbour to this Faith which
alone can ſave him, is this againſt Charity ?

To ſay, *Out of the true Church there is no ſalvation,*
is no more than what St. *Paul* teaches in his epiſtle
to the *Galatians,* (v. 20, 21.) where he numbers
hereticks among thoſe that *ſhall not obtain the kingdom
of God.* It is no more than our Saviour himſelf
ſays, in theſe words of the goſpel : *He that believeth
and is baptized ſhall be ſaved, and he that believeth
not ſhall be damned,* (Mark xvi. 16.)

Nor can it be uncharitable to ſay, that no one
can be ſaved without keeping the commandments :
If thou wilt enter into life, keep the commandments,
(Matth. xix. 17.) Or to ſay no one can be ſaved
without baptiſm : *Unleſs one be reborn of water and
the Spirit, he cannot enter into the kingdom of God,*
(John iii. 5.) So neither is it uncharitable to ſay,
that

that no one can be ſaved without the true Faith ⁚ *Without faith it is impoſſible to pleaſe God.* As one is a caution to Faith, the other is to manners ; yet ſome of theſe ſayings which exclude all ſinners out of heaven, may ſeem as uncharitable to them as others do to hereticks : but all who take offence thereat ſhould conſider, that all theſe truths the Church declares, not as from herſelf, but from the clear and expreſs word of God : How, then, is the Church uncharitable in declaring the truth of the goſpel ?

Charity flatters not, nor invents new ways to heaven ; but endeavours to aſſiſt others in the way of truth, and to retrieve them from the way of error. Charity ſeeks all good to others ; as it does when it admoniſhes them, that *without Faith it is impoſſible to pleaſe God :* and *out of the true Church there is no ſalvation.*

On the contrary, it would be very *uncharitable,* as well as *erroneous,* to ſay with a ſet of *libertines* and *politicians* (in *Luther's* days) that people may be ſaved in any Church or religion ; becauſe this would be confirming them in an error againſt that *truth* which is revealed for their ſalvation. As there is but *one God* and *one Chriſt,* ſo *but one Faith, one fold of Chriſt.* There is a wide difference between a flattering enemy, who tells you, all is ſafe even in your errors, and a charitable friend who adviſes you to haſten out of them. Charity ſpeaks the *truth,* and *rejoices at it,* (1 Cor. xiii. 6.)

EXHORTATION. As God has bleſſed you by making you a member of his Church, return him due thanks, and be inſtrumental, as far as you can, to bring others to the way of ſalvation. Pray for thoſe that err, rather than upbraid them. Admoniſh them with lenity to turn from their errors to eternal truth. Endeavour to reconcile their minds to the true religion by wholeſome admonitions, an edifying life, and pious example. C H A P.

C H A P. VII.

`On the Supremacy of St. Peter and his Successors.`

Feed my Lambs : Feed my Sheep, (Jo. xxi. 16.)

Q. WHO is the Pope, and what power has he ?
A. He is the Bishop of *Rome,* the successor of St. *Peter,* and head of Christ's Church on earth.

Q. When did Christ make St. *Peter* head over his church ?

A. When he said to him after his resurrection : *Feed my lambs : Feed my sheep,* (John xxi. 15,17.) He then gave him power to feed and govern the whole flock.

Q. To what end was the supremacy of St. *Peter* instituted?

A. That it might descend to his successors to keep peace and unity in the church of God to the end.

Q. Where did St. *Peter* die ?

A. He translated his chair from *Antioch* to *Rome,* where he died for his Faith.

Q. Did any ever challenge a succession of his supremacy ?

A. No one ever did but those who succeed to his chair, the Bishops of *Rome* ; and their claim has been confirmed by Fathers and General Councils.

INSTRUCTION. We hold then and believe, that as there never was a civil government, but what had a head or supreme power over it to do justice, to make laws and preserve peace and unity ; so in the church the same is equally necessary, that there should be one head over all other prelates to keep order and
unity

unity therein. All power and authority in both is from God, according to that of St. Paul, *Let every foul be fubject to the higher powers : For there is no power but from God, and thofe that are, were ordained by God,* (Rom. xiii. 1. and 1 Pet. ii. 13.) To obey our lawful fuperiors both in church and ftate, is an indifpenfible duty of Chriftian morality. *Therefore of neceffity be ye fubject, not only for fear of anger, but alfo for confcience fake,* (Rom. xiii. 5.) What more wholefome both to church and ftate than this doctrine?

Now; as God ever had a Church of chofen people, as well under the Old Teftament, as the New, to love and ferve him, fo he appointed a head over them : as *Mofes* and *Aaron* under the Old law, and St. *Peter* and his fucceffors in the New. This fupremacy of St. *Peter* was promifed and declared in very remarkable terms, by our Saviour in St. *Matthew,* (xvi. 16.) where this difciple having made a full confeffion of the Divinity of Chrift, he replied to him as follows. *Bleffed art thou Simon Barjona, becaufe flefh and blood hath not revealed to thee, but my Father who is in heaven. And I fay unto thee, thou art a rock ; and upon this rock I will build my Church, and the gates of hell fhall not prevail againft it : And I will give unto thee the keys of the kingdom of Heaven : And whatfoever thou fhalt bind on earth, fhall be bound alfo in heaven : And whatfoever thou fhalt loofe on earth, fhall be loofed alfo in heaven.*

What he then promifed to *Peter,* the fame he conferred upon him after his refurrection, viz. jurifdiction over the whole flock, as we read in St. *John :* (xxi. 15. &c.) *So when they had dined, Jefus faid to Simon Peter, Simon, fon of Jonas, loveft thou me more than thefe? He faith unto him, Yea, Lord, thou knoweft that I love thee. He faith unto him, Feed my lambs. He faith unto him again the fecond time,*

*time, Simon, son of Jonas, lovest thou me? He saith
unto him, Yea, Lord, thou knowest that I love thee.
He saith unto him, Feed my lambs. He saith unto
him a third time, Simon, son of Jonas, lovest thou me?
Peter was saddened, because he said to him a third
time, Lovest thou me; and he said to him, Lord, thou
knowest all things; thou knowest that I love thee: He
saith unto him, Feed my sheep.*

Here Christ gave to *Peter* the power to feed and
govern the whole flock, both the lambs and the
sheep. This is none of our private interpretation of
the text; but the unanimous doctrine of the ancient
Fathers, that our Saviour by these words appointed
St. *Peter* the head pastor over his Church on earth;
and that his supremacy descends by *divine right* to
his successors: And who are his successors, but the
Bishops of *Rome*? He translated his chair from
Antioch to *Rome*, and there he died a martyr under
Nero, and *Rome* has been the seat of his successors
ever since. I never read of any others, but the
Bishops of *Rome*, that pretended to succeed to his
supremacy; who indeed has any title to it besides.

The Fathers and Councils have unanimously acknowledged the supremacy of St. *Peter*, and his successors the Bishops of *Rome*: Noted is the saying
of St. *Jerom*: "*Among the twelve one is chosen, that*
"*a head being appointed, the occasion of schism might*
"*be taken out of the way.*" (Cont. Jovin. l. 1. c. 14.)
The first was St. *Peter*; and after him all his successors: In fact, has he not been succeeded by a
visible succession of above 240 Bishops of *Rome*, acknowledged as supreme Pastors of the Church
down to our times? It would be endless to cite at
length all the ancient Fathers, who have attested
the supremacy of St. *Peter* and his successors; but
we may save ourselves that trouble: The *Centuriators* of *Magdeburg*, rigid *Lutherans*, have done it to
our

our hands : They have in their Annals cited the Fathers both Grecians and Latins, and cenfured them for their doctrine of the fupremacy of St. *Peter,* and of the Bifhops of *Rome* his fuccessors ; which is at leaft owning the fact, that the ancient Fathers of the primitive Church did unanimoufly teach that doctrine ; the fame which Roman Catholicks now defend : (See Cent. 4. Col. 125. 555. 556. and 558. Cent. 3. Col. 84. and 85. Cent. 5. Col. 774. 777. 778. 779. 781. 782. and 823.

In the fourth Council of *Lateran* under *Innocent* III. with the confent both of the Grecian Bifhops and Latins, a decree paffed : " That the Church of " *Rome,* by the difpofal of the Almighty, holds the " principality of ordinary power above all others, " as being the Mother and Miftrefs of all faithful " Chriftians."

The decree of the Council of *Florence* is as follows :

We define that the holy Apoftolical fee and the Bifhop of Rome holds the Primacy over the whole world. And that he is the fucceffor of St. Peter, Prince of the Apoftles, and true vicar of Chrift, and head of the whole Church, and the Father and Doctor of all Chriftians. And that to him in St. Peter was given by our Lord Jefus Chrift a full power to feed, and rule, and govern the Univerfal Church."

The fupremacy of the Bifhop of *Rome* may be alfo clearly feen in the privileges, which he always enjoyed in the Church, and which are competent to none but the fupreme Paftor.

Firft ; That all Bifhops throughout the Chriftian world, who find themfelves aggrieved by their ecclefiaftical Judges, whether Provincial or National Synods or Patriarchs, may have recourfe by appeal to the Bifhop of *Rome* ; this alone fhews that he has

ever

ever been acknowledged by the Church as ſupreme Paſtor.

Secondly; That in all diſputes ariſing concerning matters of Faith, that part of Chriſtians, which has adhered to the Biſhop of *Rome* and the Apoſtolick See, holding communion with him, has ever been accounted Catholick and Orthodox ; and that part diſſenting from him, heretical or ſchiſmatical.

Thirdly; That nothing concerning Faith can be decreed and defined, ſo as to make ſuch decree effectual to the Univerſal Church, without the conſent and confirmation of the Biſhop of *Rome :* All which is a full proof that he has the government of the whole flock ; as other prelates only have of their own dioceſe or province.

In a word ; as the Church of Chriſt is a ſpiritual body diffuſed in many nations, and under many temporal Princes, to which an uniformity in Faith and Worſhip is abſolutely eſſential ; it is neceſſary there ſhould be one ſupreme Paſtor in ſuch a body, for uniting all national Churches in one Univerſal Church, they being all bound in duty to the profeſſion of one and the ſame Faith. And if it be found neceſſary in every patriarchy, in every ·national Church, and metropolitical province, to have their patriarch, their primate, their metropolitan, to keep order and unity therein, and prevent ſchiſm ; how much more neceſſary for the ſame end to have one head in the Univerſal Church ? For how can the members of the Church diſperſed in ſo many ſeveral nations and kingdoms be kept in unity, unleſs ſome head, ſome ſupreme Paſtor have authority over them all ? Since therefore God would have one Catholick Church throughout the world, it was neceſſary he ſhould appoint one head. In effect he did appoint one in the perſon of St. *Peter,* and prayed for him *that his Faith might not*
fail :

fail: But the ſupremacy of St. *Peter,* eſtabliſhed by Chriſt for the well governing of his Church, was not to die with *Peter,* no more than the Church was to die with him, but to deſcend to all his ſucceſſors, to *feed, rule* and *govern* the flock, as long as the Church ſhall endure, to the end of the world. Hence, the Fathers and Councils, and all faithful Chriſtians, have ever acknowledged the ſupremacy of St. *Peter* ſtill ſurviving in his ſucceſſors of *divine right.*

Yet the Roman Catholick Church never defined, that the Pope has authority to depoſe princes, or diſpenſe with our allegiance to lawful ſovereigns; or to licenſe ſubjects to take up arms againſt them. In the decree or definition of the Council of *Florence* for the Pope's ſupremacy, as above cited, there is no mention of any ſuch depoſing power, neither in the Creed of *Pius* IV. or in any other Creed uſed in the Roman Catholick Church. On the contrary, that Church conſtantly teaches our Saviour's command, *Render to Cæſar what belongs to Cæſar.* The Pope is ſupreme in *Spirituals,* but not in *Temporals,* except in his own principality. The Pope may interdict and excommunicate princes, even Cæſar himſelf; but it is no part of our Catholick belief, that he can deprive them of their thrones.

EXHORTATION. As the obedience of our will is a duty neceſſary to the keeping God's commandments, ſo is the ſubmiſſion of our underſtanding and judgment to make us true believers, true and perfect members of his Church. *Obey your prelates, and be ſubject to them,* (Heb. xiii. 17.) As the neglect of the firſt is the overthrow of innumerable ſouls, following their own and diſregarding the will of God; ſo is the latter the deſtruction of many, by following their own private judgment contrary to the will of thoſe whom God has placed over them.

This

This difobedience is the mother and nurfe of all *in-fidelity* and *herefy.*   O! my foul, how often have you been taught to be obedient to the higher powers both in Church and State, neither of which can fub-fift without fuch our obedience!   .

Our obedience is what the law of God requires to both: *Obedience is better than facrifice.*

Now, as God has placed a chief primate or head over his whole Church, we are all called upon 'for our obedience to him in *fpirituals.*   If by the divine law we are obliged to obey our ordinary prelates, and be fubject to them; how much more to be fubject to him, who is our prime and chief prelate? I mean the *Pope,* the fucceffor of St. *Peter,* as all true Chri-ftians have ever held.   O! remember that divine faying of Chrift to *Peter, To thee I will give the keys of the kingdom of heaven: And whatfoever thou fhalt bind on earth, fhall be bound alfo in heaven: And whatfoever thou fhalt unbind on earth, fhall be unbound alfo in heaven,* (Matth. xvi. 19.)

C H A P.   VIII.

On the Seven Sacraments.

By the Grace of God I am what I am, (1 Cor. xv. 10.)

2.   WHAT is grace?
    A. 'Tis a free gift of the divine bounty, to enable us to do good, and avoid evil, the evil of fin.
    Q. Where does God liberally beftow it?
    A. In the holy facraments, which never fail to give grace to thofe who are duly prepared to receive them.
    Q. How many are the facraments of the new law?
    A. They are feven in number.

2. Are

Q. Are all the ſeven to be held as ſacraments of Chriſt's inſtitution ?

A. Yes : They have been held as ſuch by the Latin andGreekChurch, in all paſt ages, down to us.

Q. To what end were they inſtituted ?

A. To ſanctify all ſtates of life.

Q. Which are the moſt neceſſary to ſalvation ?

A. Baptiſm and *Penance* : Theſe are called the *Sacraments of the dead,* as reſtoring them to the life of grace : And the holy Euchariſt, as preſerving the ſpiritual life in our ſouls.

Q. And are not the other ſacraments alſo neceſſary?

A. They are all neceſſary, tho' not all neceſſary to every one : (Council of Trent, Seſſ. 7. Can. 4.)

INSTRUCTION. As we are all born ſo helpleſs of ourſelves, and in a conſtant need of divine grace to aſſiſt us in every ſtate of life to perform well our duties ; where has God provided us with greater helps, than in the ſeven ſacraments, as ſo many fountains of grace derived from the paſſion and merits of Chriſt ? It is by them all juſtifying grace is begun in our ſouls, either increaſed, or recovered when loſt: (Coun. Trent, Seſſ. 7. proemium.) If we were deſtitute of theſe, we ſhould be deficient in all the good required of us : As St. *Paul* teaches : *Not that we are ſufficient of ourſelves, even to have a good thought as from ourſelves, but our ſufficiency is from God* ; (2 Cor. iii. 5.)

The ſacraments of the new law were all inſtituted by Chriſt our Lord, and are neither more in number, nor fewer, than ſeven : *viz. Baptiſm, Confirmation, Euchariſt, Penance, Extreme Unction, Holy Order, Matrimony,* (Council of Trent, ibid. Can. 1.) So the Council of *Trent* defines, and the Church has ever believed.

It

It is true, we do not find the determinate number of them set down in Scripture as in a Catechism; yet we find in the New Testament seven sacred Rites of divine Institution, as outward signs of invisible grace, to be administered for ever in the Church; and these are the seven sacraments which we profess.

The same number and the same sacraments are specified in the General Councils of *Florence* and *Trent*, in opposition to some modern hereticks, who began to dispute and deny the divine institution and efficacy of some of them : For the Church does not commonly call her Councils, and proceed to definitions in matters of Faith, till her dogmas are opposed by some heresy. All the sacraments are not of equal necessity for all : But there are two held as most necessary to salvation : *Baptism* and *Penance* : For these two confer justifying grace for remission of sins, without which the soul cannot be saved ; and therefore, these two are called *the sacraments of the dead*, that is, of such as are *dead in sin*, and are restored to the life of grace by these sacraments. The others confer an increase of grace, and are called *the sacraments of the living*, because they are only to be administered, to such as are in the state of grace, and living to God. Of these the holy *Eucharist* is the most excellent, as containing Christ himself really present therein, who is the fountain of grace, the most precious and profitable food of Christian souls, and the great preservative of their spiritual life : *If any one shall eat of this bread, he shall live for ever :* And, *the bread which I will give is my flesh for the life of the world*, (Jo. vi. 52.) In a word, the seven sacraments are necessary to sanctify all states of life, and to confer grace upon us the better to fulfil the duties required therein.

EX-

EXHORTATION. O! Chriſtian ſoul, return thanks to God for all the bleſſings and graces you daily receive through the paſſion, death, and merits of *Chriſt* : chiefly for thoſe divine fountains of grace given you in the ſeven ſacraments. Bear a due veneration, and have a great faith in them, as being inſtituted by Chriſt, and affording a never-failing help and benefit to all who receive them worthily, and with due preparation. As you are not able to do any good of yourſelf without the help of divine grace, apply to them as your reſpective ſtate and wants require.

O! how miſerable would you be without *Baptiſm* ; for ever debarred entrance into heaven! Or what dangers of damnation expoſed to without *Penance*, without a due reconciliation to your offended Maker after your manifold ſins and frailties! In what ſtarving condition would your ſouls be in, without the divine food of the holy *Euchariſt* ! How ſhall you withſtand the many perſecutors of your faith and virtue in this wicked world, without the ſtrengthening grace of the *Holy Ghoſt* given you in the ſacrament of *Confirmation* ! How can you think of dying without the divine comfort and laſt remiſſion of ſins which God gives you by *Extreme Unction.* How can the miniſters of the Church have power to do ſuch holy offices as produce ſupernatural effects in our ſouls, unleſs they receive that power from God by *Holy Order* ! Or, how ſhall married perſons be happy in their difficult and burthenſome ſtate, without a ſpecial grace and bleſſing given them by the ſacrament of *Matrimony* ! Thus has God provided divine help for all ſtates in the Church, and for all the members in it, from our coming into the world, till our departure out of it by death.

C H A P.

CHAP. IX.

The holy Eucharist.

Take ye and eat; This is my Body, (Math. xxvi. 26.)

Q. WHAT is the holy Eucharist.

A. 'Tis the body and blood of *Jesus Christ* really present under the species of bread and wine.

Q. How do you prove that the body and blood of Christ are really present in this sacrament?

A. By the word of God, as expounded by the divine authority of the holy Catholick Church.

Q. Was the real presence always held?

A. Yes: It was held by all Christians in the primitive Church; by the ancient Councils and Fathers; and never called in question for many ages.

Q. Were there not many, who have opposed it in latter times!

A. Yes: In like manner many opposed the *Divinity* of *Christ* and the *Holy Ghost.* Those who oppose the real presence as held by Catholicks, are at a loss to determine what they are to believe of this great sacrament.

Q. How so?

A. Some of them hold that the body and blood of *Christ* is present *in figure only,* as *Zwinglius.* Others, that it is present *by its virtue,* as *Calvin.* Others *by Faith,* as the *Church of England.* Others *together with the bread and wine,* as *Luther* maintained.

Q. How did the Church define against them?

A. That the whole substance of bread, by consecration, is changed into the substance of the body of Christ; and the whole substance of wine into his blood: which change is fitly and properly by the Catholick Church called *transubstantiation.* (Council of Trent, Sess. 13. cap. 4.)

Q. But

Q. But is not this making a new article of Faith ?

A. No : It is only an explanation of the truth of the myftery, as it was always believed.

INSTRUCTION. As all the revealed myfteries of Faith are above our comprehenfion ; yet Reafon as well as Faith teaches us to affent and firmly believe them all, upon the authority of God the revealer, and his Church, the Teacher of them : As we believe the world was made out of nothing by his only word *Fiat : Let it be made* ; and that the dead fhall rife to life at the very call ; *Arife ye dead, and come to judgment :* So we believe the myftery of the holy Eucharift upon his word : *This is my body : This is my blood.* The holy Catholick Church, which was taught and inftructed by the Apoftles, fo expounding it as we believe it. God requires not your comprehenfion of the myftery, but your Faith ; and has pronounced thofe happy who *have not feen, and yet have believed,* (Jo. xx.. 29)

The wonderful miracle of the loaves and fifhes, feems to have been wrought by Chrift, to prepare and difpofe the minds of his difciples to the belief of this divine myftery, which foon after he laid open to them in thefe words, *I am the living bread, who came down from heaven. If any one fhall eat of this bread, he fhall live for ever,* (Jo. vi. 51, 52.) But what was the bread, which they were to eat ? He tells them in very plain words : *And the bread, which I will give, is my own flefh, for the life of the world.* (Jo. vi. 52.) The Jews wrangled and faid, *How can this man give us his flefh to eat ?* (ver. 53.) Here we fee the unbelieving Jews were the firft that doubted of the real prefence. And what anfwer did he make to them ? How did he go about to explain his words ? Not in a *figurative fenfe,* but confirms what he had before taught in fuch a fenfe, as plainly implies a real prefence of his body and
blood

blood in this sacrament. Jesus therefore said to them ; *Amen, Amen, I say to you, unless you shall eat the flesh of the Son of Man, and shall drink his blood, you shall not have life in you,* (ver. 54.) *He that eateth my flesh, and drinketh my blood, hath life eternal, and I will raise him up to life at the last day. For my flesh is meat indeed, and my blood is drink indeed,* (ver. 55, 56.)

This truth he also revealed at his last supper, when he first instituted this great sacrament. Hear his words : *As they were at supper, Jesus took bread, and blessed it, and brake it, and gave it to his disciples, and said, Take ye, and eat, This is my body. And taking the cup, he gave thanks, and gave it to them, saying, Drink ye all of this ; For this is my blood of the New Testament, which shall be shed for many for the remission of sins,* (Matth. xxvi. 26, 27, 28.)

As they were eating, Jesus took bread, and blessing, he brake it, and gave it to them, and said, Take ye, This is my body. And taking the cup, giving thanks, he gave it to them, and they all drank thereof, and he says to them, This is my blood of the New Testament, which shall be shed for many, (Mark xiv. 22, 23, 24.)

And taking bread, he gave thanks, and brake it, and gave it to them, saying, This is my body, which is given for you : Do ye this in remembrance of me. Also the cup after he supped, saying, This is the New Testament in my blood, which shall be shed for you, (Luke xxii. 19, 20.)

The same truth is clearly and fully delivered by St. Paul, writing to the *Corinthians* about the use of this sacrament, who at the same time declares he had received his doctrine from Christ himself.---*For I received of our Lord what I delivered to you : That the Lord Jesus, the same night he was betrayed, took bread : And giving thanks, he brake it, and said, Take ye, and eat :*

*eat : This is my body, which fhall be delivered for you :
do ye this in remembrance of me. As alfo the cup,
after he had fupped, faying, This cup is the New
Teftament in my blood ; do ye this, as oft as ye fhall drink
it in remembrance of me,* (1 Cor. xi. 23, 24, 25.)

It cannot be denied, but the written word in thefe
texts is clearly expreffive of a *real prefence* ; and that
the denying of fuch a *real prefence,* as Catholicks
hold, cannot ftand together with the plain, obvious,
literal fenfe of God's word. Therefore, thofe who
deny the *real prefence,* contend, that the words of
Scripture above cited, are to be taken, not in a *literal,*
but a *figurative fenfe*; and that the Eucharift is the
body and blood of Chrift in *figure only,* and to be
taken by the receivers, only as a bare remembrance
of his death. If we afk them, by what authority
they forfake the literal fenfe of God's word, and
turn fo many plain texts of Scripture to a figure ;
they have no anfwer to make, but that it is their *Opinion,* and the private judgment of their Sect, that
fuch is the true fenfe of Scripture.

Catholicks on the contrary, take the texts of
Scripture above cited, in the obvious literal fenfe,
and believe it as a prime article of their Faith, that
the body and blood of Chrift are truly, really, and
fubftantially prefent under the fpecies of bread and
wine in this facrament, and that by the Confecration, a converfion or change is made of the whole
fubftance of the bread into the body; and of the
whole fubftance of the wine into the blood of Chrift.
If any one afk the reafon of this our belief, or why
we follow this interpretation of Scripture ; be it
known to all, that we do not follow our *private
Judgment* herein, but the authority and doctrine of
the whole Catholick Church and General Councils,
which have clearly defined it. Their authority in
thus expounding Scripture, ought to be decifive of

C

this

this controversy, as well as of the controversy of the *Trinity* and *Incarnation* against former herefies. It is true, the word *Tranfubftantiation* and *real prefence* is not found in Scripture; neither is the word *Confubftantial,*or *Trinity*, or *Incarnation,*to be found there; 'tis fufficient that the fenfe is there; of which the holy Catholick Church is the Judge by authority from God, not *private Reafon.* None but infidels will deny, but God can change one fubftance into another, as he did the water into wine at the marriage of *Cana:* fo when he faid, *Take, eat, this is my body*; he by the fame omnipotent word changed the fubftance of bread into the fubftance of his body: but it is a great misfortune, as well as a great fault, to want Faith.

EXHORTATION. O! Chriftian foul; how much are you bound in gratitude to venerate and adore this divine myftery, while the outward fign is fo vifible, the fignification fo plain, and the inftitution of it fo manifeft! For why was the Euchariſt inftituted and given to us under the forms or fpecies of fuch things as we eat and drink, but to fignify that Chrift, really prefent in this facrament, is the food of fouls? O! dive not into this or any other myftery of Faith; for nothing can perplex the mind more, than a vain fearch into them by human reafon: they are not the proper object of reafon, as being above the fphere of human reafon. As God has pronounced the word, *This is my body*; take it in that fenfe the Church in all former ages ever underftood it. The Church was inftructed from its foundation in this, as well as all other myfteries of Faith, by the Apoftles.

SECT.

SECT. II.

Objections againft the Euchariſt anſwered.

Q. WHY may not the words, *This is my body*, be taken in a figurative ſenſe? Are there not many figurative expreſſions in Scripture?

A. There are: But that is not a ſufficient reaſon why thoſe words; *This is my body* ſhould be taken in that ſenſe: The *figurative ſenſe* is not only contrary to the belief of the holy Catholick Church, but to the Lutherans alſo; that is, to the greater part of Proteſtants.

Q. Why then is the Euchariſt in Scripture ſo often called *bread*?

A. Becauſe it has the outward appearance or ſpecies of bread; and really is the *bread of heaven*.

Q. How can the ſame Body of Chriſt be in many places at one time?

A. By the omnipotent power of God.

Q. Am I not to believe my ſenſes? my ſenſes report, that the bread and wine ſtill remain in their natural ſubſtance after conſecration.

A. Your ſenſes only report, that the outward ſpecies of bread and wine ſtill remain: at the ſame time Faith and Revelation teaches, that the ſubſtance of them does not remain, but is changed into the body and blood of Chriſt: So your ſenſes are not deceived, but perceive their proper object, which is the outward ſpecies of things.

· INSTRUCTION. Many are the objections of the incredulous to annul the Faith of the *real preſence*; but as they are grounded upon *private Judgment* and uncertain interpretations of Scripture, they ought to have no weight with a well inſtructed Chriſtian, who knows that he is commanded in ſuch matters of Faith, to hear and obey the unerring Church of Chriſt. Who has given you authority to expound

theſe

thefe texts of Scripture according to your *private Opinion?* Private interpretation of Scripture never was allowed in the Church of God, neither under the Old Teftament nor the New; but under the Old law, was punifhed with death. (Deut. xvii. 12.)

Altho' fome expreffions in Scripture are *figurative*, as in parables; it is no confequence that the words of Chrift, *This is my body, This is my blood,* are figurative: he was not then fpeaking in parables, but inftituting a great facrament upon which our falvation depends; which was neceffary for the world to know; and which could only be known from his words; it was not then a time to fpeak in figures and parables, but plainly: Accordingly, his words are plain, and had led all the Chriftian world before the reformation, into the belief of the *real prefence*; and the Catholick Church in all ages paft, ever underftood them in that fenfe; and indeed moft of the Proteftants; as is demonftrated by a learned Proteftant writer in a treatife entitled, *Reafons for abrogating the Teft.* The authority of the holy Catholick Church is a fufficient argument with the well inftructed, not to give ear to the *figurative fenfe*: If you require further arguments, it is becaufe you do not believe the Church; and of fuch Chrift has pronounced, *He that believeth not fhall be condemned.* (Mark xvi. 16.)

But if you muft have other reafons, you fhall have them from Luther, he cannot be fufpected of partiality to the Roman Catholick belief. " To " turn, fays he, fuch plain words of Chrift to a " figurative fenfe, under pretext that there were " figurative expreffions in other places of Scripture, " was to open a way whereby the whole Scripture, " and all the myfteries of our falvation might be " turned to figures. The fame fubmiffion therefore " is required here, wherewith we receive the other " myfte-

" myſteries, without attending to human reaſoning,
" or the laws of nature, but to Jeſus Chriſt and his
" word only. Our Saviour ſpoke not in the inſti-
" tution, either of Faith, or of the Holy Spirit, but
" ſaid, *This is my body*; and not, that Faith was to
" make you partakers thereof: what Chriſt ſpoke
" of, was not a myſtical eating, but an oral eating.
" 'Tis true, Faith ought to be there to make it pro-
" fitable; but to ſhew that even without *Faith*, the
" word of Jeſus Chriſt had its effect, you need only
" to conſider the communion of the unworthy:
" *He that eateth and drinketh unworthily, eateth and*
" *drinketh judgment to himſelf, not diſcerning the body*
" *of our Lord.* (1 Cor. xi. 29.)
From which words Luther proving, that the true
body of Chriſt, and not *in figure only*, is preſent in
this ſacrament independently of the Faith of the receiver, he then declares thoſe to be impious, who
hold it is his body in *figure only*, by affronting Chriſt
not in his gifts, but immediately in his own perſon.
(See the hiſtory of the *variations:* vol. 1. l. 2.
numb. 30.)
In a word, Chriſt did not ſay, *This is my body in*
figure, but abſolutely, *This is my body:* and, *My*
fleſh is food indeed: and, *My blood is drink indeed*: Nor
did his Apoſtles, nor Judas himſelf object againſt it.
No General Council, Fathers, or Church, ever underſtood his word otherwiſe than in the literal ſenſe
in the primitive ages. *Berengarius* with his followers about the middle of the eleventh century, was
the firſt that taught publickly againſt the belief of
the real preſence, and endeavoured to raiſe a ſect
againſt it; pretending, as ſome Proteſtants (or rather
Preſbyterians) do in our days, that it is his body in
figure only, and a bare remembrance of his death.
But this error of Berengarius and his followers, was
condemned in no leſs than eleven councils of biſhops,

and

and at laſt retracted by himſelf; and his hereſy, like
others, had no other conſequence but to make the
truth triumphant; and the doctrine of the real preſence and tranſubſtantiation, was clearly defined at
the beginning of the thirteenth century in the fourth
Council of Lateran; and afterwards in the General
Councils of Florence and Trent. ·

But is it not expreſsly ſaid, *Do ye this in remembrance of me?*

Very true: but theſe words do by no means exclude a real preſence: on the contrary; thoſe who
hold the *real preſence*, when they receive this ſacrament, they cannot but feel a much more lively remembrance of his laſt ſupper and death, than thoſe who
only take bread and wine in memory of him. Theſe
words *Do ye this in remembrance of me*, only inform
us of the end for which we are to receive this ſacrament; viz. as a perpetual commemoration of his
death; but they are not an explanation of the fore-
going words, *This is my body*; nor do they alter their
natural meaning: Hence, it is remarkable, that two
of the Evangeliſts, Matthew and Mark, have in their
goſpels quite omitted thoſe words, *Do ye this in remembrance of me:* would they have omitted them, if
they believed them to be a neceſſary explanation of
the words, *This is my body?*

. But why is the Euchariſt ſo frequently called
bread in Scripture? I anſwer, that it is alſo ſo called
in the Roman Miſſal itſelf, even after conſecration;
panem ſanctum vitæ æternæ; for which ſeveral good
reaſons are aſſigned: firſt, becauſe it really is *the
bread of heaven, the bread of Life:* ſecondly, becauſe it ſtill retains the ſpecies of *bread*, and therefore is called *bread*, as angels appearing under the
outward ſpecies of men, are in Scripture called men.
Finally, it is called *bread*, becauſe it was made from
bread; as man is called *duſt*, becauſe he was made
out

out of duft: *Duft thou art, and into duft thou fhalt return.* But left this expreffion of *bread* fhould lead us into miftake; Chrift himfelf, at the fame time he calls it *bread,* tells us what this bread is: viz: *The bread which I will give, is my own flefh, for the life of the world.* (Jo. 6. v. 52.)

If any one afk, how the fpecies of bread and wine can remain without the fubftance? furely none but an infidel will deny, but this may be done by the fame power of God, which has fo often made angels appear under the fpecies of human bodies, when the fubftance of human bodies was not there.

Still the incredulous is not fatisfied, but objects once more, that it does not feem poffible, how the fame body can be in many places at once.

But thofe Proteftants who make this objection, fhould reflect, that their brethren-reformers the Lutherans, all believing the *real prefence,* have this objection to anfwer as well as Catholicks: As alfo thofe who believe with the Church of England, That *the body and blood of Chrift is verily and indeed taken and received by the faithful in the Lord's Supper;* which of confequence muft needs be in many places at once in their Eafter communions. But let the Proteftant learned bifhop Forbes give the anfwer to this objection. " Many Proteftants, fays he, too boldly " and dangeroufly deny, that God has power to " tranfubftantiate the bread into the body of Chrift. " 'Tis true, all own that what implies a contradic- " tion, cannot be done. But becaufe in particular " no body knows certainly, what is the effence of " every thing, and confequently, what implies a " contradiction, and what not; 'tis without queftion " a rafhnefs in any, to put limits to God's power. I " approve the opinion of the divines of Wittem- " burgh, who affert the power of God to be fo " great, that he can change the fubftance of the

" bread

" bread and wine into the body and blood of Chrift."
" And if he can make the change at one time, fo alfo
" at another in the fame facrament. (Forbes de Euch.
l. 1. c. 2.) The queftion is not, whether we comprehend this myftery of our faith, but whether it is
revealed. Now it cannot be denied by any man of
candour, that we have full as good grounds in Scripture, Univerfal Tradition, and the authority of the
Church, to believe the real prefence, as for the Trinity and Incarnation, or any other myftery of the
Chriftian Religion. The myftery then being revealed, vain philofophy muft be filent.

But muft I not believe my fenfes? It appears to
all my fenfes, and to the fenfes of all, that the bread
and wine after confecration, *ftill remain in the natural fubftances* of bread and wine.

This may feem plaufible to the unlearned ; but it
is falfe philofophy: The truth is, that the fenfible
qualities, or outward fpecies of things, not the fubftance of them, are the objects of fenfe : Thefe ftill
remain in the Eucharift after confecration; fo your
fenfes are not deceived, but perceive their proper
object. But muft we not conclude, you'll fay, that
where the fenfible qualities, or accidents, or fpecies
of things are, there alfo is the fubftance under them ;
otherwife, we can never know by our fenfes where the
fubftance of things is ? therefore, as the fpecies of
bread and wine ftill appear in the Eucharift after confecration; we have a right to conclude, that the fubftance alfo of bread and wine is there ?

In anfwer hereto, fo far may be granted, that where
our fenfes perceive the accidents, or fpecies of things,
we rightly judge the things to be there, unlefs we
have certainty to the contrary, as we have in the prefent cafe: For faith and revelation affure us, that in the
Euchar ift, the fubftance of bread and wine is not there :
If after this you perfift, that the fubftance of bread
                                                        and

and wine is there, becaufe your fenfes perceive the fpecies of bread and wine ftill remaining after confecration; 'tis not your fenfes, but your infidelity deceives you. So the Difciples who faw Angels at the fepulchre of Chrift under the fpecies of men, if they had believed their fenfes more than revelation, which affured them that thofe who appeared, were angels, and not men, they had indeed been deceived, not by their fenfes, but for want of faith.

EXHORTATION. O! my foul, renew again your faith of the omnipotent power of God, fhewn forth in the many wonders contained in the holy Euchariſt. 'Tis a work of infinite wifdom; a work of infinite goodnefs; a work of infinite power; no wonder then that it is wonderful! At the fame time, there is no truth clearer in Scripture and tradition. The fermons and other tracts of the ancient Fathers both Grecian and Latin, are fully expreffive of it, All the ancient liturgies both of the Eaftern and Weftern Church, are as clear for the real prefence and tranfubftantiation as the Roman Miffal itfelf. Let learned proteftants read them, and believe their own eyes. The General Councils of the Church define it in the fame fenfe, and in the fame words in which Roman Catholicks at this day profefs it. It was never impugned but by Zwinglians and Prefbyterians, and by a fect of unbelievers in the eleventh century. Would God fuffer his Church to fall into fo grievous an error, (as is pretended) and remain fo long therein, againft this prime facrament of the Chriftian law, and fo fruftrate the covenant made with her, *When he, the Spirit of truth, fhall come, he fhall teach you all truth,* (Jo. xvi. 23.) Is not the whole Catholick Church, to which this promife was made, to be depended on before a few ftraggling members revolted from her Faith?

O then, let the authority of God's word expounded by his holy Church, fupport your belief againft

all

all temptations: Let not *Senfe*, but *Faith* direct you to judge of this divine myftery, which is not an object of your fenfes, but of Faith: *Faith comes by hearing*, not by *fight : It is the belief of things that do not appear.* (Heb. xi. 1. & Rom. x. 17.)

S E C T. III.

On Communion in one Kind.

He that eateth this bread fhall live for ever.
(Jo. vi. 58.)

Q. I CANNOT reconcile myfelf to your practice of receiving the facrament in one kind; why is it not taken as Chrift inftituted?

A. Whether we receive in one kind or both, we fully anfwer the end of the inftitution.

Q. But does not Chrift command all to receive in both kinds?

A. No : his command at the laft Supper to confecrate and receive in both kinds, only reached to the apoftles and to the priefts, whofe office it is to offer the Euchariftick Sacrifice, which cannot be done without confecrating and receiving in both kinds

Q. How far does the command extend to the priefts in private communion?

A. No further than to the reft of the faithful.

Q. Is not communion in both kinds frequently mentioned in Scripture?

A. Yes : And there is alfo mention made as frequently of communion in one kind: *This is the bread defcending from heaven, that if any one fhall eat thereof, he may not die,* (Jo. 6. ver. 50). *If any man eat of this bread, he fhall live for ever,* (ver. 51). *He that eateth this bread, fhall live for ever.* (ver. 58.)

INSTRUCTION. The holy Catholick Church, which received from Chrift the whole power and authority of teaching the truth of his gofpel, has
de-

decreed in two General Councils, that of Conftance, and that of Trent, that it is fufficient to receive in *one kind*; feeing we believe that Chrift himfelf is really prefent in this facrament, and received under each kind: And as the grace of this facrament is wholly derived from Chrift therein really prefent, who is the fountain and caufe of all grace to us; it cannot be doubted by any one who has a right Faith in Chrift, that the fame and as much is received under one kind as both. And thus it is eafily underftood, that communion in one kind does fully anfwer the end of the inftitution. For what is the end of the inftitution of this facrament, but that by approaching to it and receiving it, we may receive Chrift, who is the food of fouls, that he may preferve life in us, till foul and body arrive to life everlafting? Now Chrift being alike prefent under the fpecies of bread, as under the fpecies of wine; whether we receive in one kind or both, we receive the fame fpiritual and immortal food of our fouls, and all the grace effential to this facrament.

Well: but fince Chrift commanded all to receive in both kinds, you cannot, as you fay, but think yourfelves wronged to be thus defrauded of the cup: Did not he fay to all, *Drink ye all of this?* · ·

This our adverfaries miftake: That command, *Drink ye all of this*, was not given to the laity. Chrift at the laft Supper gave two commands, both of them directed to the Apoftles, and in them to the priefts, not to the laity. The firft is contained in thefe words, *Do ye this in remembrance of me*; whereby he gave a command, and alfo power, to confecrate in both kinds, which is not the office of the laity but of priefts. The fecond in thefe words, *Drink ye all of this*: whereby he commanded them to communicate in both kinds as often as they fhall confecrate: Now as the firft command of confecrating in both kinds, was given only to the

the priests as is evident; and not to all the Chrisῑtian people, without diſtinction of clergy and laity; upon what grounds are you ſo confident, that the other command, *Drink ye all of .this,* was diῑrected to all the faithful, any more than the comῑmand of conſecrating expreſſed in the words, *Dʒ ye this in remembrance of me;* whereas, it is clear our Saviour in both ſpoke to none but the Apoſtles? It is certainly therefore very wrong, in theſe our priῑvate interpreters of Scripture, to apply to all the laity the command of our Saviour directed only tʒ the Apoſtles at the time he made them prieſts, and gave them power to conſecrate the holy Euchariſt; for with as much reaſon they may pretend, that he gave the laity power to *forgive ſins,* and *adminiſter baptiſm* in ordinary, and preach, when he ſaid to his Apoſtles, *Whoſe ſins ye ſhall remit, they are remitted unto them;* and when he ſaid to them, *Go ye, and teach all nations, baptizing them.*

Now, as to the command, *Drink ye all of this;* it is conſtantly fulfilled by biſhops and prieſts of the Catholick Church, as often as they conſecrate and offer the Sacrifice. But in private communions they receive as the laity, in one kind under the form of bread. Can it be thought they intend hereby *to deῑfraud themſelves of one half of the ſacrament?*

In a word, it was the practice in the primitive Church, for the laity to communicate ſometimes in *both kinds,* and ſometimes in *one:* In public comῑmunions they did commonly (tho' not in all places) communicate *in both;* in private communions, *in one.* The learned part of our adverſaries know what I here aſſert to be true; and the ſame may be eaſily proved beyond reply. This ſhews that the primiῑtive Church, which was taught and inſtructed by the Apoſtles in all matters of Faith and ſacraments, knew of no divine command for all the laity to reῑceive in both kinds,

There

There are ftatutes and injunctions in the reformed Churches themfelves, to adminifter the communion in *one kind*, to fuch of their people as have an antipathy to wine, which is fairly owning, that it is not *contrary to the inftitution and command of Chrift*; for if it were, it would be not only *a half facrament*, but a *whole facrilege*, not to be difpenfed with by the ordinance of any Church, or the act of any ftate.

As to the frequent mention in Scripture of communion in *both kinds*, there is alfo much mention therein of communion in *one*; from whence, neither you do rightly infer, that the laity communicated always *in both*; nor we, that they communicated always in *one:* But the only right inference is, that they communicated fometimes in *one*, and fometimes in *both*; it being ufual in writers, to mention the manners and cuftoms of their times, as they were commonly done.

To conclude; Is it not ftrange, that a fet of obfcure men, Luther, Calvin, and their followers, without miffion or authority from any lawful fuperior, fhould be more knowing and clear-fighted in this and other divine matters, than our primitive anceftors, and fhould now fee things wholly unfeen in all ages before ?

EXHORTATION. O Chriftian foul! as you believe and fubmit to all truths taught by the holy Catholick Church ; be you alfo obedient 'to this point of her doctrine and difcipline, grounded on the fame authority and antiquity.

As then you believe the body and blood of Chrift, even Chrift himfelf, is truly prefent under each kind, and life promifed to the receiver of either; follow the prefent practice of the Catholick Church ; authorifed by the decrees of General Councils. Prepare yourfelf to a holy communion in *one kind.* O! receive

this

this bread of heaven, remembering the word of Chrift, *that he who eateth thereof may not die.* Adore your bleſſed Jeſus equally preſent in *one kind* as *in both,* and therefore cannot fail to produce the ſame fruits and effect in your ſoul.

But no wonder thoſe are in an error about the manner of receiving this ſacrament, who are in an error about the ſacrament itſelf, and neither believe the body and blood of Chriſt is received, neither in *one kind* nor *both.* Let them firſt believe the real preſence with all orthodox Chriſtians throughout the world, and true faith will open their eyes, to ſee that the ſacrament is entire in either kind, Chriſt being entire in each. Luther indeed held, that only the body of Chriſt is preſent together with the bread, and only the blood of Chriſt with the wine, which is putting him in a real ſtate of death ; in which abſurd ſyſtem it would indeed be conſequent, that there is not as much preſent in one kind as in both. But as one abſurdity follows the other, we muſt renounce both, and thank God that has enlightened us with the true faith, whereby we know there can be no ſeparation of the body and blood of Chriſt ſince his reſurrection ; nor ſeparation of his Divine Perſon, and his human Nature, ſince his Incarnation ; and therefore he is entire in each kind in this adorable ſacrament.

When therefore you are preſent at the ſacrifice, raiſe up your heart to *both kinds,* and join with the prieſt in commemorating the death and paſſion of our Lord : O ! think how his body was crucified, and his blood ſhed for you ! Abhor that vain and arrogant doctrine, which teaches that Chriſt is only preſent in the Euchariſt *in figure,* like former hereticks, who held that he was only *in figure* upon earth before his paſſion, and not *truly* and *ſubſtantially.* Confeſs him really preſent under each kind, and adore him as your Lord and your God : *Ah ! my Lord and my God.* (John xx. 28.

.   SECT.

· 'S E C T. IV.

The Eucharist a Sacrifice.

Do ye this in remembrance of me. (Luke xxii. 19.)

Q. WHAT is the Mass?

A. 'Tis a sacrifice or offering of the body and blood of Christ, under the species of bread and wine.

Q. By whom was it instituted?

A. By Christ at his last supper.

Q. To what end was this done?

A. That the sacrifice of the cross might be daily represented before our eyes, and the memory of it ever continue; and that the blessed fruits thereof might be continually imparted to us.

INSTRUCTION. Religion is the worship of God, and this duty we fulfill in the most essential manner, by offering sacrifice to him, in acknowledgment of his supreme being, and dominion over us and all creatures. For this reason, under the law of nature, before a written law was given, God was worshiped publickly by sacrifice, by his servants and adorers, the ancient Patriarchs and their Families; Abel, Enos, Noe, Abraham, Job, Melchisedeck, who always believed that sacrifice was a necessary worship, and that it could not lawfully be offered to any other but the true God, as the law of Moses afterwards plainly taught: *He that sacrificeth to the gods shall be put to death, to any other but to the Lord only.* (Exod. xxii. ver. 20.)

Under the law of Moses, three kinds of sacrifice were appointed to be offered by the priests of that law, viz. the *Holocaust*; the *Sin-offering*; and the *Peace-offering*. But these sacrifices were only types and figures of another sacrifice to come, and were not adequate to the majesty of God. At length then

Chrift coming, and finding in the world no offering
pure enough to be offered to God, he offered himfelf
once on the crofs, and by his inftitution and command, is daily offered on the altar. Then all the
facrifices of *Aaron*, the *Holocaufts*, the *Sin-offerings*,
and the *Peace-offerings*, which were but types of this,
were to ceafe, and the only facrifice of the Mediator
to remain ; in which all perfection is found, that
can be as well in the facrifice as in the facrificer :
now, that this facrifice may never ceafe, the priefts
are commanded to do what Chrift did at the laft fup-.
per fo to *announce the death of the Lord till he cometh*,
(1 Cor. xi. 26.) Thus the facrifice of the crofs
and the altar has fulfilled in truth, all that was figured
by the ancient facrifices ; this one anfwering the end
of them all ; as being the moft perfect *Holocauft* of
divine love : The true *Peace-offering*, and *propitiation for fin*; and the moft acceptable *thankfgiving*
that can be offered to God for all his benefits.

This daily facrifice was plainly foretold by the
prophet Malachy, in thefe words : *My will is not
with you, faith the Lord of hofts, and I will not accept an offering at your hands: for from the rife-
ing of the fun unto the fetting thereof, great is my
name among the Gentiles. And in every place facrifice
is offered to my name, and a pure offering: becaufe great
is my name among the Gentiles, faith the Lord of hofts,*
(Malachy i. 10, 11.)

In this prophecy, God rejects the facrifices of the
Jews, and fubftitutes in their place another pure and
holy facrifice to be offered to his name all the world
over among the Gentiles. 'Tis evident, this cannot
be the *bloody* facrifice of the crofs, becaufe that was
only offered once, and in one place ; this which is
foretold by the prophet, to be offered *from the rifing
of the fun to the fetting thereof in all places.* What
then is this *pure offering*, but the facrifice of the altar,

which

which being the ſame hoſt that was once offered on
the croſs, is truly moſt *pure* and *holy.* This is the pure
offering foretold by Malachy, which has been for ſo
many ages offered to *the name of God in every place* by
the converted Gentiles. Accordingly, the primitive
Doctors of the Church, St. Juſtin, Iræneus, Tertullian, and Cyril of Alexandria, apply this prophecy
of the euchariſtick ſacrifice, and teach in expreſs
terms, that the apoſtles learned from Chriſt, to offer
this ſacrifice throughout the earth. (See Juſtin. Dial.
cum Tryphone. Tertull. con. Marcionem, lib. 3.
c. 21. Iron. lib. 4. c. 32. Cyril con. Jud. lib. 2.
12. 16.)

· But is it not written, that Chriſt *offering up one
ſacrifice for ſin, there is no more oblation for ſin,* (Heb.
x. 12 & 18.)

It is true, there is but *one ſacrifice of redemption,*
viz. that of Chriſt upon the croſs ; God required but
once the ranſom paid ; and this is the ſacrifice of
redemption St. Paul ſpeaks of, where he ſays, there is
no more oblation for ſin : the redemption wrought by
his ſacrifice on the croſs was *an eternal redemption.*
Yet as his prieſthood was not to be extinguiſhed by
his death, but ever to continue *according to the order
of Melchiſedeck;* he left a viſible ſacrifice to his Church;
viz. his body and blood, under the ſpecies of bread
and wine, which he offered to his eternal Father at
the laſt ſupper, and delivering it to the apoſtles to partake thereof, he commanded them, and in them the
prieſts their ſucceſſors, to offer the ſame by theſe
words, *Do ye this in remembrance of me ;* that ſo
by this offering, his ſacrifice on the croſs may be
daily repreſented before our eyes, and the memory
of it continue to the end of the world: And as
in this divine ſacrifice of the altar, the ſame Hoſt is
offered as on the croſs ; well may we believe that it is
a truly *propitiatory ſacrifice* ; and that the remiſſion of
ſins,

fins, and the fruits of that moſt wholſome ſacrifice of
our redemption on the croſs, are plentifully imparted
daily to all devout adorers by this of the altar; ſo far
is this from derogating from the merit of the other :
at the ſame time, by this divine ſacrifice we render
ſupreme worſhip and due honour to God upon his
altars *in all places*, as the prophet foretold; and all
the faithful are united in one publick worſhip. (See
Coun. of Trent, Seſſ. 22. c. 1, 2.)

If our adverſaries object, *That every prophecy of
ſcripture is not of private interpretation.*

This we grant; nor do we interpret the prophecy
of Malachy, as proteſtants do, by our *private interpretation* : but in this and other texts of ſcripture,
relating to the euchariſt both as a *ſacrament* and *ſacrifice*, we follow the public interpretation of the
church and fathers : " For ſo the holy Catholick
" Church ever underſtood and taught," as the council of Trent obſerves. (Seſſ. 22. c. 1.)

As to the fathers, the moſt eminent proteſtant
writers, after they had diligently examined their
writings on this head, at length fairly owned, that
theſe ancient doctors taught the euchariſt to be a
ſacrifice, as well as a *ſacrament*, to be offered to God
all over the world. " It cannot be denied, ſays
" Rempnitius, a rigid proteſtant, but the ancients,
" when they ſpeak of the celebration of the Lord's
" ſupper do uſe the word *ſacrifice, immolation, oblation,*
" *hoſt, victim.*" (Exam. Con. Trid.)

Luther alſo, after an exact ſcrutiny of the fathers
ſentiments, at length puzzled how to expound them
in favour of his reform, bids farewel to them all in
theſe words : " If there is nothing more to be ſaid,
" it is ſafer to deny all, than to grant that the maſs
" is a ſacrifice."

To Luther, we may add Calvin, who gives up
the fathers to us as roundly as Luther : " I ſee,
" ſays '

" fays he, that the ancients alfo turned this memo-
" rial to a different purpofe than is fuitable to the
" inftitution of our Lord; inafmuch as their fupper
" carried the face of I know not what, repeating and
" renewing of a facrifice." (Inftitut. l. 4. c. 18.
& 11.)

The Centuriators of Magdeburgh alfo, who were
rigid *Lutherans*, confefs that the primitive Fathers
taught this our Catholick doctrine of the Euchariftick facrifice.

(Cent. 2. c. 4. col. 63) They blame St. Irenæus for teaching this fame doctrine. " Of the
" Oblation, fay they, Irenæus feems to fpeak im-
" properly enough, when he fays, That Chrift
" taught a new oblation of the New Teftament,
" which the Church receiving from the Apoftles,
" offers to God all the world over."

(Cent. 2. c. 24. col. 63) They likewife blame
St. Ignatius Martyr, for the fame doctrine.

(Cent. 3. c. 4. col. 83) They cenfure St.
Cyprian for teaching, " That the prieft officiates
" in the place of Chrift, and that a facrifice is
" offered to God the Father."

From the teftimonies of all thefe proteftant writers, proteftants themfelves cannot but conclude,
that thefe moft ancient primitive Fathers held the
Eucharift to be a facrifice of divine inftitution ;
and what they taught in their dogmatical writings,
the fame was in practice all over the Chriftian
Church, as all the ancient liturgies at this day extant bear witnefs. Let but our adverfaries in-
fpect, and read over the liturgy of St. James; that
of St. Clement; that of St. Bafil; and of St. John
Chryfoftom; that expounded by St. Cyril of Jerufalem; and that by St. Ambrofe; the Armenian;
the Coptick; &c. in every one of them they will
find a *rule* or *canon* prefcribed for the offering this
facri-

sacrifice of the body and blood of Chrift under the species of bread and wine, for the living and the dead, expreffed in as full terms as in the Roman Miffal. The mafs then is as ancient as Chriftianity: And with good grounds, both from Scripture and tradition, did the Council of Trent define: *That therein is offered to God a true and propitiatory facrifice both for the living and the dead.* (Seff. 22. Can. 1. & Can. 3.)

EXHORTATION. O Chriftian, praife God in all his wonderful works, chiefly in the holy Eucharift, which by his inftitution he has made both facrament and facrifice: In the one, to be the fweet food of our fouls; in the other, that we may give to God due *adoration* and *thankfgiving*; that we may have Chrift prefent on our altars to *intercede* for us; and to expiate our daily fins. His love and goodnefs is fo great, as not only to yield up his life once on the crofs for our redemption; but he would ftill continue to be our facrifice on the altar for the fins of mankind, by daily imparting the benefits of his death and paffion, to fuch as are there prayed for and recommended, whether living or dead, by the prieft that offers; Chrift himfelf, who is the Hoft, interceding for them: *Ever living to intercede for us,* as St. Paul fays, (Heb. vii. 25.) he is the true Mofes, ftill diverting the fcourge of heaven from us.

O think yourfelves moft happy under fuch a divine Holocauft! never fail attending thereat; but let it be with a pure heart, with a *contrite heart*; with interior *adoration*, devout *thankfgiving*; and fervent *prayer* and *fupplication*; ftill renewing the memory of his death, which is commemorated in this daily facrifice, and by which the merits and fruits thereof are plentifully imparted to our fouls. Say then, *Lamb of God, who takeft away the fins of the world, have mercy on us.*

SECT.

S E C. T. V.

On the Latin Liturgy or Mass in the Latin Tongue.

2. WHY is the mass and the divine office in your Catholick Church celebrated in the Latin tongue, and not rather in the vulgar tongue of every country?

A. To keep up an uniformity in the divine worship in all places; and to avoid the changes that the vulgar languages are subject to.

2. But would it not be more edifying to the people, especially the ignorant, in a language which they understand?

A. The liturgy in the vulgar tongue of every country, would be attended with great inconveniencies: neither is it so very requisite; seeing the priest at mass is not *preaching,* but *praying,* and offering sacrifice for the people; and they are otherwise instructed in the meaning of this sacrifice.

2. How can the ignorant and illiterate be made to understand the meaning of a Latin service?

A. 'Tis the pastors care to instruct them from their infancy: Besides, the mass is translated into many of the vulgar languages, and inserted into common prayer books: Not indeed for the lay people to recite the canon along with the priest, but only to inform them and their protestant neighbours of the meaning thereof, that they may the better join with the priest by devotion and consent.

2. But how can they join with the priest in what they do not understand?

A. 'Tis sufficient their intention goes along with him in commemorating the death of Christ: God does not so much regard the *lips* as the *heart.*

INSTRUCTION. The Catholic Church never held it as a necessary rule, that the liturgy should

be

be celebrated in a language *unknown* to the people. This is evident; becaufe from the beginning her liturgy was chiefly in Greek and Latin; in Greek for the eaſt; and in Latin for the weſt; which were the languages the moſt univerfally underſtood in thofe times. Yet neither did ſhe judge it convenient or neceſſary, that it ſhould be celebrated publickly in the vulgar tongue of every country: This is alfo evident; for tho' Greek and Latin in the primitive ages of the Church were. the moſt univerfal languages; yet they were unknown tongues to very many of the vulgar people in moſt nations, who had their peculiar language, and knew and fpoke no other; notwithſtanding, the Church never indulged them with the liturgy in their vulgar tongues, but ſtill kept it in the learned languages: For which many very good reaſons are affigned.

Firſt, becaufe the learned languages being fixed by the rules of grammar, are not liable to thefe changes and corruptions as the vulgar languages are. Secondly, to keep an uniformity in the publick worfhip of God in all parts of the Church, tho' ever fo widely diſtant; for now, thofe that travel into foreign countries, finding there the liturgy in the fame language as at home, if they are prieſts, they can officiate; if not, they can attend it with the fame devotion as in their own country. But in the reformed Churches, where the liturgy is allowed in the vulgar tongue of every country, they are *barbarous* in refpect to one another, all reading and praying in *unknown tongues*, underſtood generally by none but the natives of each particular country. With good reaſon then the Council of Trent did not think fit to decree, that the maſs ſhould be celebrated commonly in the vulgar tongue of every country. (Seff. 22. c. 8.) Not to keep the vulgar in ignorance: Nothing is more groundleſs than

that

that afperfion ; for the Council at the fame time in-
joins all paftors to inftruct their people diligently in
their vulgar tongue, in every point of the liturgy :
Is this keeping them in ignorance? Thus the illiterate receive no prejudice by the liturgy being celebrated in the Latin tongue, they being well inftructed
in the meaning thereof, by their paftors, and by many
excellent writings publifhed for that purpofe. They
are taught that the prieft at the altar, by the inftitution of Chrift, is offering facrifice for them, and that
the facrifice is *propitiatory both for the living and the
dead:* 'Tis fufficient that they join with him by confent and devotion, tho' they neither underftand, nor
fo much as hear the words of the canon, or offering;
which by the rituals of all the liturgies both of the
Eaftern and Weftern Church, is ordered to be reci-
ted *in fecret* by the prieft that officiates, as being his
proper office.

And as in the time of the old law it was fufficient for the people who ftood out of the temple, and
were out of the fight and hearing of the prieft that
offered the facrifice, (Luke. i. 10.) fufficient, I
fay, for them to know that he was offering facrifice for them, and to join in heart and intention
with him; fo now it fuffices for the Chriftian people
to be prefent with devotion, and join with the offering by confent, tho' they neither fee nor hear the
prieft at the altar, which muft be commonly the cafe,
efpecially in all great Churches. Even the deaf,
blind, and dumb, may be made fenfible of what is
doing for them in the divine fervice.

As to the other parts of the divine office of the
Church in Latin, what offence can it give ? Seeing
the people at the fame time pray in a language which
they underftand, and the prieft prays for them in a
language which he underftands: Yet even herein the
people may join by their devotion, as they well know
the

the Church office confifts of pfalms, and hymns, and other moft devout prayers: And if the cfilence of prayer *is an elevation of the heart and mind to God*; no one, I think, need be afraid of glorifying God by joining in the divine office, tho' he underftands not the language.---So thofe religious communities of women repeating the divine office in Latin, tho' many of them underftand not the language perfectly, I doubt not, receive great benefit by joining with the choirs of the Church, and the choirs of Angels in praifing God, who does not fo much regard the mouth as the heart and intention. He is more honoured by the *heart* than the *lips*.---As to inftructions, fermons, exhortations; thefe throughout the whole Catholick Church, are always delivered in the vulgar tongue of every country.

EXHORTATION. As you are fufficiently inftructed and underftand the meaning of the divine facrifice, which is offered to God *in all places*, as the prophet Malachy foretold; join daily with the prieft in commemorating the death and paffion of our Lord. Reflect well on what he fuffered for you in the garden; in the feveral courts of Annas, Caiphas, Herod, Pilate, and on the crofs.

And as the prieft is not *preaching* but *praying* for you, join your intention with his, while he offers the facrifice *for all who are prefent with devotion*: He offers it as a *divine Holocauft*, to give to God that fupreme adoration which is due to him. Adore God then at the fame time *in fpirit and truth*. Return *thankfgiving* and praife for all bleffings received: Supplicate for pardon of your fins thro' this facrifice *of propitiation*. And let your *petitions* be made known to God thro' Jefus Chrift, who on the altar is both prieft and facrifice. Every time you fhall attend on this divine fervice with devotion, the merits and fruits of his paffion will redound to the good of your
foul.

foul. Pray for all who are blind to this myftery: There are none fo blind as thofe who will not fee the great Myfteries of our Faith.

C H A P. X.

On Penance, and Confeffion of Sins to a Prieft.

Whofe fins ye fhall remit, they are remitted unto them.
(Jo. xx. 23.)

Q. WHAT do you mean by *Penance ?*

A. Penance, which before the coming of Chrift was no Sacrament, is now made a Sacrament of divine Inftitution, by which all fins committed after Baptifm are remitted to true penitents.

Q. What is required on the part of Penitents for this remiffion of fins ?

A. To be contrite of heart: To confefs their fins to the Prieft. And to perform the fatisfaction or penitential works enjoined. Thefe are the difpofitions required of Penitents : But the Abfolution is given by the Prieft ; and the grace that juftifies the finner given by God.

Q. By what power does the Prieft act ?

A. Not by any power of his own, but by the power of Chrift, which he imparted to the Apoftles, and to thofe who fucceed them in the Priefthood.

Q. When was this power given them ?

A. When after his Refurrection he breathed on them, faying, *Whofe fins ye fhall remit, they are remitted unto them ; and whofe fins ye fhall retain, they are retained.* (Jo. xx. 23.)

Q. Was this power given to any others but the Apoftles ?

D

A. Yes ;

A. Yes; as I faid, it was undoubtedly to pafs to their Succeffors. As when he gave them power to *Preach, Baptize,* and *Confecrate* ; who can doubt but that power paffed to thofe who fucceeded them by a lawful *Election, Ordination,* and *Miſſion ?*

Q. It feems as if you made Gods of your Priefts ; for the power of forgiving fins only belongs to him.

A. No more than Chrift our Lord made Gods of the Apoftles, when he gave them this power : Cannot God make men the inftruments of his power ; as he did Moyfes and Aaron under the Old Teftament, and his Apoftles under the New ?

Q. Is it not enough to confefs to God ?

A. Before Penance was made a Sacrament, it was fufficient. But now Confeffion both to God and the Prieft is made neceffary ; becaufe we live under a law that requires it ; and at the fame time gives the Prieft power to abfolve us in the name of God.

Q. Is not Confeffion to a Prieft, and Abfolution as held by Catholicks, an encouragement to Sin ?

A. Quite the contrary : For Confeffion is a great reftraint to nature ; and many conditions are required to a valid abfolution ; *viz.* A fincere examine of confcience, and Confeffion of every mortal fin to the Prieft ; a hearty forrow for them ; and a real purpofe of amendment ; with fatisfaction for fins paft.

INSTRUCTION. " Penance was not a Sa-
" crament before the coming of Chrift, nor fince
" his coming to any one before Baptifm. But
" Chrift our Lord then in particular inftituted
" the Sacrament of Penance, when after his Re-
" furrection from the dead, he breathed on his
" Difciples, faying, *Receive ye the Holy Ghoſt* ;
. " *whoſe*

" whofe fins ye fhall remit, they are remitted unto
" them; and whofe fins ye fhall retain, they are
" retained. By which remarkable action, he gave
" to his Apoftles and their lawful Succeffors, the
" power of remitting and retaining fins, for the
" reconciling of the Faithful, who fall into fin
" after Baptifm : So the Fathers unanimoufly ever
" underftood it : And the Catholick Church with
" great reafon, formerly condemned and explod-
" ed the Novatian Hereticks, who denied this
" power of remitting fin." So far the Council
of Trent : (Seff. 14. chap. 1.) And the fame
Council has pronounced *Anathema to thofe who fhall
fay, that Penance, as ufed in the Catholick Church, is
not truly and properly a Sacrament, inftituted by Chrift
our Lord, for reconciling the Faithful as often as they
fall into fin after Baptifm.* (ibid. Can. 1.)

We hold then two effential truths : Firft, That
Baptifm is neceffary for remiffion of Original Sin,
and all fins committed before Baptifm. Secondly,
That Penance is a Sacrament neceffary for remiffion
of fins after Baptifm. By *Baptifm* we have the firft
remiffion : By *Penance,* the Second. For fince men
are fo frail, as all muft know, and as apt to
fall into fin after Baptifm as before ; it was neceffary the Church fhould have another Sacrament of
divine Inftitution, befides Baptifm for remiffion of
fins after Baptifm ; feeing, that without remiffion
of fins the foul cannot be faved.

Hence God, rich in mercy, knowing this our
frailty, has provided a remedy for all, who are fallen again under the power of the devil, and the
flavery of fin, fince their Baptifm, to reftore them
again to the life of Grace : And this remedy is the
Sacrament of Penance, which by applying the benefit of Chrift's death, remits all fins to fuch as
are truly penitent. (Coun. Trent, feff. 14. chap. 1.)

'There

There is no fin nor finner, if penitent, excepted. What an unfpeakable comfort to all fuch! How melancholy and miferable the condition of thofe who acknowledge not this truth! Who have no Sacrament for remiffion of fins after Baptifm; but live and die in their fins without this remedy! They believe in the firft remiffion of fins by Baptifm; and why not in the fecond by Penance? Is not the fecond as effential and neceffary for the falvation of the foul as the firft? Is it not a truth acknowledged by all, that without the forgivenefs of fins, the foul cannot be faved? And is not the divine Inftitution of the Sacrament of Penance, and the Prieft's power of abfolving, as clear in the Gofpel, as Baptifm, and his power of Baptizing? Of the one it is written: *Go ye; teach all Nations, baptizing them in the Name of the Father, and of the Son, and of the Holy Ghoft.* (Matth. xxviii. 19.) And, *Unlefs a man be reborn of water and the Holy Ghoft, he cannot enter into the Kingdom of God.* (Jo. iii. 5.) Of the other, it is written: *Receive ye the Holy Ghoft; whofe fins ye fhall remit, they are remitted unto them; and whofe fins ye fhall retain, they are retained.* (Jo. xx. 23.) Yet, the Prieft abfolves in the name of God, and by the authority of God, not by any human power: *I abfolve thee from thy fins, in the Name of the Father, and of the Son, and of the Holy Ghoft.*

2. But why is it not enough to confefs to God?

A. Let St. Auguftin give the anfwer: "In vain," fays he, "did Chrift fay; Whofe fins ye fhall remit, "they are remitted unto them, if it were fufficient "to confefs to God only; it would fruftrate his "words, and the truth of the Gofpel." Confeffion of fins to the Prieft, is therefore neceffary for this reafon, becaufe we live under a divine Law that requires

quires it. Hence the Council of Trent defines, that it is neceſſary by *divine right*, to the remiſſion of ſins, for all the Faithful who are fallen into ſin after Baptiſm, to confeſs to the Prieſts all and ſingular mortal ſins, even the moſt hidden, and ſuch as are only againſt the two laſt commandments of the Decalogue, with all the circumſtances that change the nature of the ſin; as far as they can remember, after a diligent examen of their conſcience; and the Council pronounces *Anathema* to thoſe who ſay the contrary. (Seſſ. 14. c. 5. & Can. 7.)

Some ſtill object further: That at this rate it is ſufficient to run to a Prieſt, and confeſs even the greateſt crimes, and believe all is well: Thus conſeſſion to a Prieſt encourages ſin.

On the contrary, I will ſhew, that it is the greateſt curb to ſin, inaſmuch as it puts the greateſt reſtraints on a ſinful nature: For many conditions are required to a good Confeſſion and a valid Abſolution: As firſt, a ſerious examen of Conſcience, of the number and weight of our ſins; ſecondly, a hearty ſorrow and deteſtation of them; thirdly, a ſpecial Confeſſion of them to the Prieſt, which is a great act of ſelf-humiliation; fourthly, a firm and real purpoſe of amendment; laſtly, a faithful performance of the penance enjoined. Now, let all reflect whether theſe, which are no eaſy duties, are encouragements to ſin. Nay, tho' Confeſſion were a mere human political act, it would be a great reſtraint upon many exceſſes committed by man: But as it is a Divine Act, and a Sacrament which gives grace, it is ſo far from promoting ſin, that it is the moſt powerful help to overcome it. At the ſame time it gives the greateſt comfort to Penitents, reconciling us again to our offended Maker and Redeemer. This is the voice of God to all that repent

D 3.   and

and confefs : *Whofe fins ye fhall remit, they are remitted unto them.*

In a word, we have the fame grounds for our belief of the divine inftitution of the facrament of Penance, as for Baptifm : *viz.* The word of God expounded by the authority of the holy Catholick
Church, formerly againft the Novatian Hereticks,
and fince in her General Councils ; as in the fourth
of Lateran, of Florence, and Trent, againft the
fectarifts of latter times.

EXHORTATION.   Praife God, O Chriftian !
in that divine Power which he gave to his Apoftles.
and their Succeffors by thefe words : *Whofe fins ye
fhall remit, they are remitted unto them.*   Have recourfe to it as your neceffities fhall require.   As the
bleffing is great, great is your obligation of humbling
yourfelf under the divine juftice, and the divine
mercy.   Seeing your foul is ftained with many im-
pieties ; confefs them both to God and his Minifters,
as penitent David did to Nathan ; that you may hear
thofe comfortable words : *I abfolve thee from thy fins,
in the Name of the Father, Son, and Holy Ghoft ;*
whereby you are juftified in the fight of God.

But remember, you come with the conditions required for Abfolution : To wit, a good confeffion ;
a contrite heart ; a fincere purpofe of amendment ;
a ready will, to fulfill the penitential works enjoined
by the Prieft.

God has done, and ftill continues to do great
wounders by man, efpecially by his Minifters.   As
in Baptifm he purifies the foul by water, and thofe
words of his Minifter : *I baptize thee in the Name
of the Father, and of the Son, and of the Holy
Ghoft :* So in the Sacrament of Penance, by thefe
words of the Prieft : *I abfolve thee from thy fins,
in the Name of the Father and of the Son, and of the
Holy Ghoft :* He figns and feals our pardon in heaven.

ven. Both are done by the power of God committed to his Minifters; they by his inftitution adminiftering the Sacraments; and he at the fame time, by the fame giving the interior grace, and effect thereof.

Delay not then your repentance, but embrace the prefent time of mercy, and be converted to the Lord your God, before his juft wrath and indignation overtake you. Reflect well, repent well, before you prefent yourfelf at the throne of divine mercy, that your fins may be blotted out. Judge yourfelf, that you may not be judged.

C H A P. XI.

Of Indulgences.

Whatfoever thou fhalt unbind on Earth, fhall be un-bound in Heaven. (Matth. xvi. 19.)

Q. WHAT do you mean by an Indulgence?
A. 'Tis a releafing of the temporal punifhment due to fin, after the guilt thereof has been remitted by the Sacrament of Penance.

Q. By what power does the Church remit this temporal punifhment due to fin? The punifhment is fuppofed to be due by the divine juftice; how can the Church releafe it?

A. By authority from Chrift, who has given this power to his Minifters.

Q. What is required to the gaining the benefit of an Indulgence?

A. That we be in the ftate of grace; and that we perform the good works enjoined by the authority that grants the Indulgence.

Q. But do not thefe Indulgences encourage fin?

A. On the contrary, they are the caufe of the converfion of many.

IN-

§ 4. INSTRUCTION. An Indulgence is a remiſſion of the temporal puniſhment, which remains due to our ſins, after the guilt thereof is remitted by the Sacrament of Penance. This was practiſed by St. Paul, in the caſe of the inceſtuous Corinthian : For we read that the Apoſtle mitigated the Penance he had laid upon him; and forgave him *in the Per-ſon of Chriſt*, as he terms it; that is, by the authority of *Chriſt*, and this he did at the requeſt of the Faithful, and becauſe he judged that ſuch an Indulgence would be more for the good of the penitent's ſoul, than the ſeverity of Penance; *leaſt he might be abſorbed with over-much ſorrow*, (2 Cor. ii. 7. and 10.) And in this ſenſe we find this grant of Indulgences to have been much practiſed in the primitive Church; which by it's Conſtitutions and Canons having enjoined very long and ſtrict penances for great ſins, eſpecially when ſcandalous, left it however to the diſcretion of the Biſhops in their reſpective diſtricts to diſcharge penitents, from a part or the whole of their penance, either in conſideration of their fervent repentance and change of life, or, in time of perſecution, at the interceſſion of the martyrs; or in a word, when they judged that the good of their penitents ſouls required it; and this is what we call *an Indulgence*.

To make this the more clear, we muſt diſtinguiſh two things in ſin; the guilt thereof; and the debt of puniſhment we owe to divine juſtice for it. Now, upon the ſinner's repentance, and an humble Confeſſion, joined to the Prieſt's Abſolution, Faith teaches, that the ſin is remitted as to the guilt and the eternal puniſhment due to it; but that God ſtill reſerves a temporal puniſhment, or penance, to be undergone by the ſinner in this life; as well to make ſome amends to injured mercy, as to caution him againſt future relapſes: And as there are but few that

that

that do all the penance required; to make up this deficiency, Indulgences are granted by the Church, requiring other good works of penitents, and so acquitting them of the whole penance due.

To this our adversaries object: That no punishment or penance remains due to sin, after it is remitted; for how is the sin truly remitted, if the punishment of it still remains?

We answer: That when we say the sin is remitted, we mean the guilt thereof, and the eternal punishment due to it; this is properly, *the remission of sin*, according to the usual stile of Scripture. Yet the same Scripture teaches, that after the sin is thus remitted, still some penance is to be done. Every one may convince himself of this truth, by what we read of the penitent David; that altho' upon his sincere repentance, the prophet Nathan pronounced his pardon: *The Lord also hath taken away your sin:* (2 Kings xii. 11. and 19.) Yet the Prophet denounced to him many heavy temporal chastisements; and the same threaten other sinners; for which there is no remedy, but either to do penance, or sue for mercy by an Indulgence. God forgave David's sin; yet inflicted many temporal punishments upon him for it; and tho' David knew by revelation, that his sin was forgiven, he still thought himself under an obligation of doing penance in this life. But God's indulgence to us is greater: For he not only remits the guilt of our sins, by the Sacrament of Penance, but also, the temporal punishment due, by a *plenary Indulgence.* In a word, what mean those frequent exhortations and admonitions of Holy Scripture, calling upon sinners to do works of penance? and what mean the Canons of the primitive Church, enjoining those penitential works to repenting sinners, (which is also the practice of the present Church, in the administration of the Sacrament of Penance) but in order to

cancel

cancel the debt of temporal punishment, due to their
sins already confessed ? 'Tis this temporal punishment or penance, that remains due to sin after the
guilt thereof, and eternal punishment is remitted to
penitents, which is released by an *Indulgence*; if we
devoutly perform the conditions and good works enjoined to those who have power to grant it.

This power is not from man, but from God himself, saying, first to St. Peter, and afterwards to all
the Apostles, *Whatsoever you shall bind on Earth, shall
be bound also in Heaven*; *and whatsoever you shall unbind on Earth, shall be unbound also in Heaven.*
(Matth. xvi. 19. and xviii. 18.) But since we do
not argue upon our own *private judgment* in this, or
any other controversy, let us see what the General
Council of Trent has decreed of this matter of faith,
as follows :---" Seeing the power of granting In-
" dulgences was given to the Church by Christ ;
" and the Church, in the most early ages, did
" make use of this power, as received from him,
" the most holy Synod teaches and commands, that
" the use of Indulgences, which is highly beneficial
" to the Christian People, and approved of by the
" authority of the sacred Councils, shall be retained
" in the Church; and condemns and anathematizes's
" those who either pronounce them unprofitable, or
" deny the power of the Church to grant them."
(Coun. Trent. Sess. 25. Decree of Indulg.)

To the validity of an Indulgence is required :
First, That it be granted by a lawfull authority :
And secondly, That there be a sufficient cause or
motive for the grant of it. On the part of those
it is granted to, many conditions are also required :
As Confession of sins to a Priest; Communion of
the holy Eucharist, Prayers, Fastings, Alms; in a
word, all the good works enjoined by those who grant
the Indulgence, must be diligently performed to
gain this remission or pardon.

This

This well confidered, 'tis not fo eafy a thing as our adverfaries pretend, to gain the benefit of an Indulgence : Great humiliation is required thereto. Sin is not fo foon remitted, nor its punifhment, but by fincere acts of penance. Neither does the Indulgence take off the general obligation of leading a penitential life, which is the indifpenfible duty of every Chriftian. *Do worthy fruits of penance, do penance,* is faid to all : To the juft, to preferve them from fin ; to finners, to avert the indignation of God. (Matt. iii. 8. & iv. 17.)

The Indulgence then granted by the Church, if rightly underftood, and not *mifreprefented,* as it commonly is by our adverfaries, can never encourage to fin, but rather invites to a total converfion from fin : feeing the Church at fuch times earneftly exhorts all finners to return to God with their whole heart ; and to encourage them to the good works enjoined for the gaining the Indulgence ; fets open all the treafures of divine grace, propofing the moft ample rewards that God promifes to all thofe, who by a fervent repentance fhall become objects of his mercy. All this joined together, we may well hope, cannot but end in the converfion of many finners ; and alfo encourages the multiplying of good works in the fouls of the faithful, which is the chief intent of the Church, at leaft, one great motive for granting thefe Indulgences. And tho' the good works required for obtaining the benefit of a *Plenary Indulgence,* if confidered fingly as the works of each perfon, may feem but inconfiderable ; yet when taken alltogether as done by the faithful in a body ; they are very great, and of great merit ; and fufficient to bring down great bleffings upon the world.

No doubt but Indulgences as well as other good things may be abufed : But that is no reafon why
the

the divine inftitution of them, which *is highly beneficial to the Chriftian people,* fhould be given over.
Had Luther directed his invectives only againft the
abufes, and prefled the reformation of them in a canonical way; he had deferved no blame, but praife.
But proceeding to attack the power of the Church,
and the divine inftitution itfelf of Indulgences, fhews
he was not directed by an humble but proud fpirit,
which directed him at length to the overthrow of
all faith and religion. In a word, the Church at
that time was fo far from countenancing fuch a-
bufes, that fhe ufed all the remedies in her power
to redrefs them. The Council of Trent in particular, after the example of former Councils,
made a decree, that moderation fhould be ufed in
the grant of Indulgences, according to the ancient and approved cuftom of the Church. And
that all fordid gain in the difpenfing of them,
which had been the caufe of thofe abufes, fhould
be entirely abolifhed. (See Seff. 25. Decree of Indulgences.)

Thefe then, in fum, are the truths we hold :
'That there is a power left to the Church by Chrift
our Lord, of granting Indulgences : That the
Paftors of the Church by his power, do apply
the merits of his Paffion and Death to acquit
our indebted fouls of the temporal punifhment,
which remains due to the divine Juftice, after the
guilt of fin is remitted by the facrament of Penance; which is called an *Indulgence.* And we do
not doubt but thofe who have recourfe to fuch Indulgences, do prevent many heavy temporal judgments
falling on their heads.

Indulgences fo underftood, are evidently an encouragement to repentance and good works, and have
made many faints; why then fhould they not make

many

many penitents ; since so many acts of Penance are required to the gaining the benefit thereof ?

EXHORTATION. Give due praise and thanks to God, who in his mercy has ordained such means, as not only remit sin, but also the temporal punishment due to it.

As you are a sinner, bound in many debts to the divine Justice ; fail not to embrace those blessed Indulgences granted you by a divine power and authority. But see you come with just dispositions to the obtaining of them ; with a sincere, pure, and upright heart ; and punctually perform all the good works enjoined. How many by them have obtained a general pardon, and prevented many temporal punishments ? Take then these words spoke to St. *Peter* and his successors as from the mouth of God : *Whatsoever thou shalt bind on earth, shall be bound also in heaven : And whatsoever thou shalt unbind on earth, shall be unbound also in heaven.* (Matt. xvi. 19.)

C H A P. XII.

S E C T. I.

On Purgatory..

If any man's work burn, he shall suffer loss ; but himself shall be saved, yet so as by fire. (1 Cor. iii. 15.)

Q. WHAT do you mean by Purgatory ?
A. A middle state of souls ; wherein such as depart this life in the state of grace, but have not fully satisfied for their sins, are detained till they have made full satisfaction, and are purified from every stain ; because *nothing defiled can enter heaven.* (Revel. xxi. 27.)

Q. Is

Q. Is the word *Purgatory* found in Scripture?

A. No: But the fenfe, or thing fignified by it, is there.

Q. How do you prove a Purgatory?

A. By Scripture and tradition, as expounded by the holy Catholick Church, not by private Judgment.

Q. Does not the preaching of Purgatory make people bold in fin, and neglect repentance?

A. No: It does not; for nothing is more frequently taught and urged to the Faithful in the Catholick Church, than the neceffity of a true repentance?

Q. What is the punifhment inflicted in Purgatory;

A. As to the kind of punifhment, or length thereof; the Church has defined nothing.

INSTRUCTION. Our doctrine of Purgatory is contained in the definition of the Council cf Trent. " That there is a Purgatory, and that the
" fouls detained therein are helped by the fuf-
" frages of the Faithful, efpecially by the accepta-
" ble facrifice of the altar. - And the holy Synod
" enjoins the bifhops, to fee that the wholefome doc-
" trine of Purgatory, as delivered down from the
" Fathers and facred Councils, be believed and held
" by the Faithful in Chrift, and every where taught
" and preached. But what is uncertain, and has the
" look of falfehood, let them not permit to be pub-
" lifhed or handled." (Coun. Trent. Seff. 25. Decree of Purg.)

The fame doctrine was defined by the Council of Florence, a hundred years before Luther preached the reformation. Subfcribe to this, and the Catholick Church preffes you no further. As to what fome bold writers have publifhed of a *material fire* burning fouls for fuch a term of years, or months, or

days;

days; aſſigning the place on the *confines of hell*; and
aſſerting that the *pains* of Purgatory are not different
from thoſe of hell, only as to their *duration*; theſe
are no articles of Faith, nor is any one obliged to
believe them. The doctrine of our Church chiefly,
as it is ſtated in her creeds and definitions of her Ge‑
neral Councils, and her practice conformable to that
doctrine, is the whole we undertake to defend, not
the extravagant flights of every private writer.

We believe that all who die in a ſtate of perfection
and ſanctity, paſs immediately after death unto bliſs.
And that all who die in the ſtate of deadly ſin with‑
out repentance are carried forthwith to hell, from
whence there is no redemption. Now, we have
reaſon to believe, that the number of thoſe is but
ſmall in compariſon, who lead ſuch holy lives, and
die ſuch holy deaths, as to be tranſlated immediately
after death from this vale of miſery to the regions of
bliſs. And yet we cannot think, that all who are
not of this rank of the perfect, are ſo unworthy as
to be caſt forth into utter darkneſs: This would be
a very deſpairing maxim, for which there is no re‑
medy but the belief of a *Purgatory*, a *third place*, a
middle ſtate of ſouls after death, as Catholicks hold.
Let St. Auguſtin explain this point of our belief:
" 'Tis not to be doubted, ſays he, but that the ſouls
" departed are relieved by the devotion of their living
" friends, when the ſacrifice of the Mediator is of‑
" fered, or alms given for them in the Church.
" Theſe are a relief to ſuch ſouls as in their life-time
" deſerved to have this help after death."

" When the ſacrifice of the altar, or alms, are
" offered for all the Faithful departed: For ſuch as
" are very good, they are a thankſgiving offering.
" For ſuch as are not very bad, they are a propiti‑
" ation. For ſuch as are very bad, tho' they are
" no

" no relief to them, yet they are some kind of com-
" fort to the living." (Euchirid. c. 109

Purgatory is proved from the words of St. Paul :
*If any man's work shall burn, he shall suffer loss; but
he himself shall be saved, yet so as by fire.* (1 Cor.
iii. 15.) Also from the words of Christ in St. Matthew: (c. xii. ver. 32.) *He that speaketh against the
Holy Ghost, it shall not be forgiven him, neither in this
world, nor in the next.* From whence St. Augustin
observes, that some sins are forgiven in the other
world. Not in heaven, nor in hell; therefore
in a *third place.* But not till divine justice be satisfied; for God is just to punish sin in the other world
as well as in this: Those penitents, therefore, who
have neglected to do that penance here which his
justice requires, will suffer there till justice be satisfied, and their souls purified from every stain of sin
before they can enter heaven.

As to the word *Purgatory* which is so offensive to
the ears of some, 'tis only a term made use of by
the Church, to explain her belief of this middle state
of suffering souls, where they are purified. And tho'
the word be not in Scripture, the thing signified by it
is therein taught. So other mysteries of our Faith
are explained in the creeds by words not found in
Scripture, as the *Trinity, Consubstantiality, Incarna-
nation.*

Against a Purgatory, our adversaries object these
words from Scripture: *If the tree fall to the South,
or to the North, in whatever place it shall fall, there
it shall be.* Eccles. xxxi. 3.)

Some imprudently conclude from these words,
that all souls which depart their bodies, are translated immediately either to heaven, or to hell; and
so there is no third place. But the words in the
text import no more, but that every soul at death
finds itself in an unchangeable state either of salvation.

·tion or damnation, which argues nothing againſt
Purgatory; becauſe the ſouls that are there, are in
one of thoſe two ſtates, to wit, in the ſtate of ſalvation, and their deſtiny to eternal bliſs is immoveably
fixed.

They object again, the words of the Apocalypſe:
Bleſſed are the dead who die in the Lord: From hence-
forth, ſays the Spirit, they may reſt from their labours;
for their works follow them. (c. xiv. ver. 13.) Does
not this import that there is no Purgatory after death
for ſuch as die in the ſtate of grace? For how do
they reſt from their labours in ſuch a ſuffering
ſtate?

To this may be anſwered: That this text is moſt
properly underſtood of thoſe who die in a ſtate of
ſanctity and perfection, for theſe are the bleſſe! that
die in the Lord, according to the uſual ſtile of
Scripture. Yet it is verified alſo in thoſe that
are in purgatory; for even ſuch as are ſecure of their
ſalvation, they are happily paſſed over all dangers;
they are delivered from all fear of damnation; they
are got ſafe out of the hands of all enemies and perſecutors: And tho' they are in a ſuffering ſtate, they
ſuffer with the comfort of angels, as knowing their
ſufferings will end in glory: Such may be well ſaid
to reſt in a good degree from their labours.

But did not Chriſt die for our ſins? And did he
not by his death make full ſatisfaction for them?
What need then of *penances*, *indulgences*, or a *pur-*
gatory to ſatisfy for ſin, when 'tis allowed by all,
that nothing can make an adequate ſatisfaction for it
but his merits and death?

In anſwer we ſay; That tho' Chriſt died for our
ſins, he ſtill requires that we apply the merits of his
death to our ſouls by the ſacraments, penitential
works, and other means which he has appointed:
Otherwiſe we may leave off the practice of all ſacraments,

craments, and doing good works, under pretence that Chrift died to gain heaven for us; what need then of any more? A maxim evidently erroneous and pernicious. He who made us and redeemed us without ourfelves, will not fave us without ourfelves; but requires that we co-operate with his grace. As he inftituted baptifm to free us from original fin; fo he ordained penance to cancel the fins we commit after baptifm.

As faith teaches that none are forgiven without baptifm; fo neither fhall we be forgiven if we neglect penance: *Unlefs ye do penance, ye fhall perifh alike.* (Luke xiii. 5.) Tho' Chrift has fatisfied for our fins, he has not thereby freed us from the obligation of doing penance for them; *but he fuffered for us, leaving us an example, that we might follow his fteps.* (1 Pet. ii. 21.)

In a word; the Scripture is not to be interpreted neither by the private Judgment of Catholicks, nor of thofe that diffent from them; nor the myfteries of Faith to be defined by human reafoning, but by the authority of the holy Catholick Church. By following the doctrine and authority of that Church, the world became Chriftian; and by following the fame, the Faithful in all paft ages have been preferved from all the herefies and errors of the times. Now, our Catholick doctrine of a Purgatory has been defined in no fewer than three General Councils; viz. In the fourth of Lateran, (c. 66.) In that of Florence, (Decret. de Purg.) and in the Council of Trent, (Seff. 25.) Likewife, in all the ancient liturgies of the Church that are extant, a commemoration and prayers for the dead has its place. The fame belief and practice is much recommended in the writings of the primitive Fathers: In fhort, there is not a more unanimous and univerfal tradition of the Chriftian Church for any point of Faith, than for our

belief

belief of Purgatory, and our practice of praying and ſacrificing for the dead ; as ſhall be proved in the next ſection.

EXHORTATION. O my ſoul, adore God in all his divine attributes, but chiefly for his great mercy and juſtice here met together, both to puniſh and to pardon; thus to prepare thoſe ſuffering ſouls to enjoy him in glory: Here juſtice and peace have truly embraced each other: O bleſſed divine attributes of God !

Theſe ſouls in Purgatory are detained there only for a time ; they ſuffer in the height of charity; yet it is a great torment to them, to be deprived of the ſight and poſſeſſion of God, which they ſo eagerly thirſt after. Be punctual then in this life to confeſs your ſins, even to the leaſt and ſmalleſt imperfections. Embrace all the works of Penance and Indulgence, which may preſerve you from this purging fire. Take all the evils of life as your purgatory and juſt puniſhment of ſin. Accept of them as from the hand of God's mercy with the greateſt ſubmiſſion, and in the height of love and charity, that ſo you may eſcape the hand of divine juſtice hereafter.

S E C T: II.

Praying for the Dead.

'Tis a wholeſome and holy Cogitation to pray for the Dead, that they may be looſed from their Sins. (2 Macch. xii. 43.)

Q. WHAT warrant have you to pray for the dead?

A. The words of Scripture above cited, which ſpeak clearly for it without ambiguity, and recommended it to the living.

Q. The

Q. The books of Macchabees are not among the canonical books of Scripture; what authority have they?

A. Although some modern scripturists have excluded them the canon, they were put therein by the primitive Church.

Q. What other grounds have you for praying for the dead?

A. From the practice of the Church in all past ages, from the positive doctrine of the ancient Fathers and Tradition; and the decrees of General Councils.

Q. How do you know that prayers can be availed for the dead?

A. By the same reason as we know our prayers are a help to the living: We no where find the dead excepted from the benefit of them.

Q. But how do you know the souls you pray for, are in want of your prayers? or suppose they are in hell?

A. If those we pray for in particular, are not in the *Middle State*; yet it is an act of charity and mercy on our part; and acts of charity cannot go unrewarded.

INSTRUCTION. As the Church teaches us to believe a purgatory, the same authority teaches us, that the souls detained there are helped by our prayers, alms, and chiefly by the offering of the divine Sacrifice of the altar: We quote the book of Macchabees for this truth; where we read, That *Judas Machabeus collected and sent twelve thousand drachmas of silver to Jerusalem for sacrifice to be offered for the sins of the dead; and thinking well and religiously of the resurrection; for unless he hoped those who were fallen would rise again; it might seem a superfluous and vain thing to pray for the dead. It is therefore a whol-*

*a wholeſome and holy cogitation to pray for the dead;
that they may be looſed from their ſins.* (2 Macch.
xii. 41. 42. 43.)

That the books of Macchabees were held for canonical Scripture in primiiive times, St. Auguſtin is
witneſs: he cites them for true Scripture himſelf,
(Lib. 18. de Civ. Dei, c. 37. and C. l. de cura pro
Mort. c. 7.) As alſo does St. Cyprian before him,
(Ep. 55. ad Cornet.) They were in the Canon
ſettled by Innocent I. In that of the third Council of Carthage: and in that ſettled by Pope Gela-
ſius. Upon the grounds of ancient tradition, they
are admitted as canonical by the Council of Trent.
The Jews have ever admitted them as a continuation
of the ſacred hiſtory, and have ever retained the practice of praying for their dead.

. The ſame is an univerſal tradition of the Chriſtian
Church: It is found in all the ancient Liturgies;
defined in three General Councils; the fourth of
Lateran, Florence, and Trent. 'Tis clearly taught
alſo in the writings of the primitive Fathers.

Tertullian, one of the moſt ancient, deſcribing the
manners of a faithful widow, ſays: " She prays
" for the ſoul of her huſband, and begs a refreſh-
" ment for him, and keeps his Anniverſary." (L. de
Monoq. c. x.)

The ſame doctrine is taught by St. Chryſoſtom:
" Oblations for the dead, ſays this Father,
" are not in vain, nor prayers, nor alms. The
" Holy Ghoſt commanded all theſe things, that
" we may help one another." (Hom. 21. in Act.)
" The Apoſtles did not enjoin theſe things in vain,
" that in the venerable and tremendous myſteries,
" the dead ſhould be remembered: they knew they
" would receive no ſmall benefit by it. For, whilſt
" all the people ſtand with arms expanded, as well
" as the prieſts, and the aweful ſacrifice is preſent,
" how

" how can it be otherwife but that we pacify God
" by praying for them ? This I fpeak of the Faith-
" ful departed." (Hom. 3. in Phil.)

" Let us therefore help them, for we have
" before us the expiatory facrifice of the world.
" Wherefore, we afk confidently for all : and name
" them with the Martyrs, Confeffors and Priefts.
" For we are all one body, tho' fome members be
" brighter than others : And it may be that we
" may obtain 'a total pardon for them, by prayers,
" by oblations, and by the Saints who are named
" along with them." (Hom. 41. in 1 Cor.) So far
St. Chryfoftom.

St. Cyril of Jerufalem is alfo very clear in this
point : " Laftly, fays he, We pray for all that die
" amongft us, believing it to be the greateft help
" that can be for their fouls, to have the holy and ve-
" nerable facrifice to plead for them." (Cat.
Myft. 5.)

But none more explicit and clear than St. Auguftin. " By the prayers of the holy Church, fays
" this Father, and the wholefome facrifice and
" alms, it is not to be doubted but the dead are fo
" far helped, that God deals more mercifully with
" them than their fins deferve." (Serm. 127. or
32. de verb. Do.)

In another place he fays : " We read in the book
" of Macchabees, that facrifice was offered for the
" dead : and tho' it were not read of in the Old
" Teftament, the authority of the Church, which
" is clear in this point, is of no fmall weight;
" where in the prayers of the prieft to our Lord
" God at the altar, the recommendation of the
" dead has its place." (De cura pro mort.)

But what need to cite any more of the Fathers
to clear this point of tradition, when Calvin himfelf fairly owns it : " That above thirteen hundred
" years

" years ago (now above fifteen hundred) it was a
" received cuftom, that fupplications fhould be
" made for the dead." (Inf. l. 3. c. 5. fect. 10.)
Kempnitius alfo, a rigid Lutheran, confeffes, that
the doctrine of praying for the dead was taught by
Origen, Ambrofe, Prudentius, Jerom, Auguftin,
Epiphanius, and Chryfoftom. (Exam. Can. Trid.
p. 3. & p. 93. & p. 107.)

Mr. Thorndike, an eminent proteftant writer of
the Church of England, not only acknowledges,
that praying for the dead is an ancient tradition,
but alfo that the doctrine is true : " The prac-
" tice of the Church, fays he, in interceeding for
" them at the celebration of the Eucharift is fo ge-
" neral, and fo ancient, that it cannot be thought
" to have come in upon impofture; but that the fame
" afperfion will take hold of common Chriftianity."
(Juft Weights and Meafures, c. 16.)

Bifhop Forbes likewife, a prelate of the Church
of England, much approves this practice : lend an
ear to what he fays of it : " Let not the ancient
" practice of praying and making oblations for the
" dead, received throughout the univerfal Church
" of Chrift, almoft from the time of the Apoftles,
" be any longer rejected by proteftants as unlawful
" or vain : let them reverence the judgment of the
" primitive Church, and admit a practice ftrengthen-
" end by the uninterrupted profeffion of fo many
" ages : and let them in public as well as private,
" obferve this rite, altho' not as abfolutely necef-
" fary, or commanded by the divine law, yet as
" lawful, and likewife profitable, and as always ap-
" proved by the univerfal Church ; that by this
" means, at length a peace fo earneftly defired by
" all learned and honeft men, may be reftored to
" the Chriftian world." (Difcourfe on Purgatory.)
Some object, that we do not know, but the
fouls

fouls we pray for in particular, may be in heaven, not in purgatory, and therefore stand in no need of our prayers.

We answer; that though it should happen we should pray for a father or mother, or friend, when they are in heaven, not knowing what state they are in, yet our work of mercy is the same, and will not fail to be available to ourselves : It is better that prayers for the dead should super-abound, than be wanting.

But suppose the fouls we pray for are irretrievably lost in hell, may we pray for such ? If not, how can our practice be vindicated praying for all that die in our communion ?

To this we reply: That as the inward state of fouls at the hour of their death is unknown to us, we suspend our judgment in a case wherein God is the only judge, and we let charity prevail, which always hoping the best, prays for all that die in the true faith : knowing that if those we pray for are uncapable of such relief, our prayers will not be lost ; but in that case, *my prayers will return into my own bosom.* (Psal. xxxiv. 14.)

But after all, is not this doctrine of Purgatory, and praying for the dead, apt to make people bold in sin, and neglect repentance ?

I cannot see any grounds for this reflection. Perverse people indeed may abuse truth as they do other good things : But why any person living should so easily and deliberately resign themselves to the pains of Purgatory in hopes of being relieved in them, we cannot comprehend. Moreover, the same Catholick Church, which teaches a Purgatory, preaches home the necessity of repentance ; teaching her people, that those who are *bold in sin,* and neglect penance, will never come to Purgatory, but descend into hell. If some libertines do

not

net observe the doctrine which is taught them ; this ought not to be imputed to their belief of a purgatory, but to their living in defiance of hell: are such only to be found where purgatory is taught ?

Let us conclude then, to pray both for the living and the dead; 'tis one of the works of mercy. Prayers and sacrifice offered for the dead, are a comfort as well to their surviving friends as to them. As all the faithful are of one church and communion, so all partake of one another's prayers and good works : If the living partake, why not the dead ? We no where find the dead excepted from the benefit of them. They are members of the same Church with us, though in a different state. Death, which dissolves the union between foul and body, cannot dissolve the union between the Head Christ Jesus and his mystical Body the Church, nor the union between the Members of that body. Souls departed then, are still fellow-members of the Church with us, and capable of being relieved by our prayers and good works,

EXHORTATION. As praying for the dead has been the constant doctrine of the Christian Church from the beginning, and the practice of it, is confirmed by Scripture, Fathers, and Councils, what can be more presumptuous than to oppose this constant universal tradition ? O ! fail not in this great work of mercy. Pray for all the faithful departed in general, and for your deceased friends in particular. Look upon them still as your brethren ; think you hear them cry aloud for relief : *Remember me, O ye my friends at least ; because the hand of the Lord hath stricken me.* (Job xix. 21.) If it be a great act of charity to help your distressed neighbour in life, in prison, in chains, in banishment and captivity, how much greater is it to assist those suffering souls under the hand of

E divine

divine juftice, who are not in a ftate to do any thing to help themfelves!

Befides, great benefit will accrue to your own foul by this pious practice: for each one will receive benefit by the prayers of the Church after his deceafe, in proportion as he has been charitable in praying for the dead in his life-time. Praying for the dead alfo puts you in mind and admonifhes you of death at the door: *Me to-day, and you to-morrow.* This will make you reflect that you muft foon follow them. But withal be careful to prepare yourfelf againft that day, by a life of penance and good works; this will make your time eafy, and your end happy.

C H A P. XIII.

On the Honour due to Saints and Angels.

S E C T. I.

Let Honour be given to whom Honour is due.
(Rom. xiii. 7.)

Q. IS there an honour due to Saints and Angels?

A. Yes: there is an honour due to them.

Q. What is the honour due to them?

A. Not *divine honour,* but fuch as we read in holy writ was given by the fervants of God to Saints and Prophets, and to Angels when they appeared to them?

Q. What are the honours in particular which Catholicks pay to canonized Saints?

A. 1. We invocate their interceffion in our publick prayers and offices. 2. We fet up their images

ges and pictures in our churches, and venerate them. 3. We visit their sepulchres, and expose their relicks to the veneration of the people. 4. We enroll their names in the calendar of Saints.

Q. Are not these extravagant honours?

A. No: They are no more than is due to such glorious persons.

INSTRUCTION. We are here to consider what honour is due to Saints and Angels; for that some honour is due to them, is no longer disputed by any, but a certain sect of fanaticks, who make no distinction between *civil honour, and divine.* Now, as to the honour due to Saints and Angels, we read in Genesis of Abraham *bowing down to the ground* to the Angel that appeared to him. (Gen. xviii. 2.) And of Lot doing the same honour to two angels appearing to him. (Gen. xix. 1.) Also, of Joshua falling prostrate on the ground to reverence one of those glorious spirits in the field of Jericho. (Josh. v. 15.) We read again in scripture of the same honour being done to Saints; that Abdias, a holy man, and one of the princes in the kingdom of Israel, fell prostrate on his face to honour the prophet Elias; at the same time Abdias in civil power and dignity was the greater person: it is therefore manifest, that he did that honour to Elias on account of his being a prophet and a saint. (3 Kings xviii. 7.) And we read again of *the sons of the Prophets* doing the same honour, to the prophet Elizeus. (4 Kings ii 15.) Now it must be granted, that the honours here given to Angels and Saints were something more than bare *civilities*; and were given them upon a religious motive; and yet were infinitely inferior to *divine worship*: unless we will make Idolaters of Abraham, Joshua, Elias, and the Saints and Angels here mentioned.

Honour

Honour is given to others on account of ſome excellency above us ; as *power,* *ſuperiority,* *learning,* *virtue.* Hence, different is the honour we give to a *parent* ; to a *king* ; to a *maſter* ; to the *virtuous* ; as Ariſtotle remarks. (9 Eth. c. 2.) And God being infinitely above all ; and the Saints and An-gels in heaven excelling and outſhining all the dignities upon earth ; there ſeems to be an ho-nour due to them as much above *civil honour,* as they by the eminency of their ſtate are raiſed above mortal men ; and as far inferior to *divine honour* as God is above them.

Some think the honour done to canonized Saints in the Catholick Church, are *extravagant* ; but they are not ſo. They may indeed be thought too great for mortal men, and are fit only for Saints in hea-ven. The honour due to the Saints in heaven, is ſurely ſomething more than civil honour which men commonly give to one another upon earth. We ſhould conſider that the Saints in heaven are crown-ed for their heroic virtues by God himſelf ; and are in a much more eminent ſtate in his kingdom, than any earthly king or citizen of this world. Yet what are the honours we give to Saints in com-pariſon with that mentioned in the *Revelations.* *He that ſhall overcome, I will grant him to ſit with me on my throne.* (c. iii. ver. 21,) But in truth, neither the honour which is done to them in heaven, nor any other which is given them by the Church on earth, is *divine honour,* but infinitely inferior to it.

SECT. II.

On the Invocation of Saints.

I believe the Communion of Saints.

Q. WHAT do you mean by the Invocation of Saints?

A. We mean no more but to beg of them to intercede to God for us.

Q. Is it not a diſhonour to God to be thus continually addreſſing your petitions to the Saints inſtead of directing your prayers to him.

A. No: It is no diſhonour to God; but on the contrary, petitioning the Saints to pray for us, is in effect praying to him.

Q. But is it not putting more truſt in them, and leſſening the confidence I ought to have in God?

A. No: It is true, I put more truſt in them than in myſelf; but all my hope and theirs alſo is in God alone. I only beg they would join their interceſſion with my petition to him, the Author of all bleſſings.

Q. What need of this, now the *Mediator* is come, and all may find acceſs to the throne of mercy through him?

A. Even ſince the *Mediator* is come, as well as before his coming, you own it was ever lawful and profitable to recommend ourſelves to the prayers of the devout, and to the Saints we live with, why not to the Saints in glory? This is no injury to the Mediatorſhip of Chriſt.

Q. But how can you know that the Saints and Angels hear your petitions?

A. Even

A. Even as we know they rejoice at the converfion of a finner.

Q. Upon what do you ground your belief and practice of the Invocation of Saints?

A. Upon Scripture, and the Authority of the Church, and Tradition; not upon *private judgment.*

INSTRUCTION. As to the Invocation of Saints, the doctrine of the Catholick Church in this matter of Faith, is contained in the following decree of the Council of Trent.

" The holy Synod commands all Bifhops, and
" all others who have the charge and care of teach-
" ing, diligently to inftruct the faithful ; firft, con-
" cerning the Interceffion and Invocation of Saints ;
" and concerning the honouring of Reliques ; and
" the lawful ufe of Images, according to the prac-
" tice of the Catholick and Apoftolick Church, re-
" ceived from the primitive ages of Chriftianity,
" and according to the confent of the holy Fathers,
" and the decrees of the holy Councils ; teaching
" them, that the Saints now reigning together with
" Chrift, do offer their prayers to God for men ;
" that it is good and profitable to invoke them with
" humble fupplication, and to fly to their prayers,
" aid and affiftance, for the obtaining the benefits of
" God thro' his Son Jefus Chrift our Lord, who is
" our only Redeemer and Saviour." (Seff. 25.)
This is the definition of the Council of Trent, condemning, at the fame time, as impious, thofe who teach the contrary doctrine, and who condemn the Invocation of Saints, as idolatrous.

Here then is our belief, as it ftands in the decree of a General Council, feparate from all mifreprefentation : From which it is evident, that we do not addrefs ourfelves to the Saints, as if they were the authors and difpofers of pardon, grace, and falvation ;

tion ; or as if they had any power to help us independently of God and the mediation of Chriſt. Hence all our prayers, even when we addreſs ourſelves to God by the interceſſion of the Saints, end and conclude, *thro' Jeſus Chriſt our Lord.* Can God be wronged hereby in any kind ? when all the hope we have by the interceſſion of the Saints is center'd in God, and in the merits of Chriſt the Redeemer.

A miſtaken notion poſſeſſes the minds of many, that invoking the Saints ſo frequently, is a leſſening of the honour of God ; but nothing is more groundleſs. As it is no diſhonour to God, to call upon the Saints and Angels in heaven, to praiſe and glorify God ; ſo neither is it to call upon them to pray for us. For if praying to God is an act of religion, and an honouring of him ; we ſtill add to this honour, when we call upon his Saints to pray with us and for us, and ſo increaſe the number of his adorers. And again, if our humble ſupplications to God be an acknowledgment of his ſovereignty over us, and of our entire dependence on him ; then certainly, when we invocate the Saints to fall down before his throne and pray for us, it is an acknowledgment of his ſupreme dominion, as well over them as ourſelves : It is acknowledging, that he is above all the Principalities and Powers in heaven, and that the brighteſt Cherubin, and the moſt exalted Seraphin, and the moſt glorious among the Saints, are his humble ſuppliants, and have nothing of their own to beſtow ; but muſt obtain all of God for their clients thro' Jeſus Chriſt : So far are we in this act of the Invocation of Saints, from making them our Gods. In a word, if it be not injurious to God to have recourſe to the prayers of the *Juſt* on earth, neither is it to call upon the Saints in heaven to intercede for us, now they are truly the *Juſt,* eſtabliſhed in grace and happineſs, pure of

all

all corruption, and moft acceptable in the fight of God.

Add hereto, that all our prayers, even when they are addreffed thro' the interceffion of the Saints, are in effect directed to God, and in him alone is all our hope for the grant of them. If you have a bounty to afk of the King, and get your petition prefented to him by fome dignified perfon who is in his favour, is not your petition, neverthelefs, made to the King? In like manner, all our prayers are made to God, tho' offered to him by the Saints interceding for the grant of them. It is not therefore true, that we truft more in the Saints than in God, but only that we place more confidence in their interceffion, than in our own unworthy prayers.

Still our adverfaries object, that there is no need of the interceffion of Saints, now the Mediator is come, and all have free accefs to God thro' him.

This, if a good reafon for laying afide the invocation of the Saints in heaven, fhould equally induce all Chriftians to give over the practice of recommending themfelves to one another's prayers: Yet this we have ever been taught, and the more holy the perfons are whom we befpeak to pray for us, the more earneft are we to partake of their prayers; knowing, *that the conftant prayer of the juft man prevaileth much.* (James v. 16.) Why then fhould we not defire their prayers, when they are crowned in heaven, and are fo near to the throne of God? If fuch interceffions on earth are not thought needlefs, why is the interceffion of the Saints in heaven to be thought needlefs? For tho' the *Mediator* is come, the end of his mediatorfhip was not to overthrow *the Communion of Saints,* in praying for one another; and there is no more injury done to the mediatorfhip of Chrift, in begging the interceffion

aeffion of the Saints above, than the prayers of the Saints on earth; this is evident: For we firmly believe, that as well thofe in heaven, as thofe on earth, have no bleffings to difpenfe independently of God, but muft obtain all of him who is *the giver of all good and perfect gifts,* thro' Chrift their *Mediator* as well as ours. They are not therefore *Mediators* in the fame fenfe as he, becaufe they ftand in need of another Mediator to recommend their petitions; and he is ftill the *only Mediator,* fo as to need no other *Mediator.*

But do not we in our offices and prayer-books invoke the Virgin Mary and the Saints, for grace and falvation, and the pardon of fin, in as full terms as we can afk them of God himfelf? Is not this making Gods of them?

To this we anfwer: That the general addrefs of Catholicks to the Virgin Mary and the Saints is, *Pray for us.* This we make the *Key* to underftand our whole doctrine of the Invocation of Saints: And as this turns them all into humble fuppliants to God, (which deftroys all notion of their divinity) it cannot be fuppofed, or in the leaft fufpected, that by any of thofe expreffions in our offices and prayer-books, we intend to equal them with God. We have a decree of a General Council (*Trent*) to regulate our doctrine and practice of the Invocation of Saints, which clearly teaches, that the Saints in heaven help us no otherways, but by their interceffion to the Lord and God of them and us: The fenfe of our Invocation of Saints, being thus for ever fixed by the publick doctrine of the Church; all expreffions in offices and prayer-books muft be underftood by that rule; and fo all Catholicks, if they will be Catholicks, underftand them. All our Invocations of the Virgin Mary and the Saints, ftill

E 5. amount

amount to no more, but, *Holy Mary, pray for us. St. Peter* and *Paul pray for us.*

That the Saints and Angels in heaven hear or know our prayers, we may learn from these words of Christ, *There shall be joy in heaven over one sinner doing penance. So I say to you, there shall be joy before the angels of God, over one sinner doing penance.* (Luke xv. 7, 10.) If they know our repentance, why may they not know the contents of our petitions when we apply to them to intercede with God to work and bring about our conversion and repentance? It is all one, whether they know this by a special revelation from God, or by that clear vision which is competent to their state of bliss. Why must we confine their knowledge to the celestial Spheres?

If some of the prophets, as we read in scripture, knew the sayings and doings of men, at a great distance from them, by the *light of Prophecy*; why cannot the Saints in heaven know the same by *the light of glory?* Why must you measure their hearing and knowledge by your own, as tho' they cannot hear beyond such a distance? you own that the devils know what is done in this world, and can hear the petitions of their impious votaries; must we then attribute more knowledge to the wicked spirits, than to the blessed spirits? In a word; we know from scripture, that the Angels pray for us, as may be learned from the prophet Zachary, who represents *an Angel praying to the Lord of hosts for the cities of Jerusalem and Judah*: (Zach. i. 12.) And that the Saints in heaven perform the like office of Angels for us, may be proved from Revelations, (v. 8.) Where we read of *twenty-four Elders* offering to God the prayers of the Saints or the Faithful. 'Tis sufficient to know that they pray incessantly for us, especially for those who call upon them; and that

God

God knows all and singular the petitions of every one that implores their intercession.

Our doctrine and practice of the Invocation of Saints agrees also with what we profess in our Creed of *the Communion of Saints.* All who are in this Communion partake of the good which is done by the members of it, and of their prayers to God ; and are not the Saints in heaven in the Communion of Saints, and do they not pray for us? If while they lived on earth, they were such zealous advocates for their clients, are they less zealous for them now they are in heaven ?

The same doctrine and practice is also agreeable to the ancient Fathers : I need not cite them at length, because our adversaries themselves freely own this truth. " I confess, says Mr. Fulk, that Am-" brose, Augustin, Hierom, held Invocation of Saints " to be lawful; and that in Nazianzen, Basil, and " Chrysostom, mention is made of the Invocation " of Saints." (Rejoinder, p 5.)

The Centurists also of Madgeburgh, though rigid Lutherans, own the fact, that the primitive Fathers held this our Catholick doctrine ; and they alledge several examples of this our doctrine and practice of calling upon the Saints in heaven to intercede to God for us, from the writings of Athanasius, Basil, Nazianzen, Ambrose, Prudentius, Epiphanius, and Ephrem, charging also St. John Chrysostom's Liturgy with Invocation of the Virgin Mary. (Cent. 4. Col. 295. & Cent. 5 Col. 675. c. 6.) Hear Mr. Thorndike, another eminent Protestant writer : " It is confessed, says he, that the " Lights both of the Greek and Latin Church, " Basil, Nazianzen, Nyssen, Ambrose, Jerom, " Augustin, Chrysostom, both the Cyrils, Theo-" doret, Fulgentius, Gregory the Great, Leo ; " more, or all after that time have spoken to the " Saints,

" Saints, and defired their affiftance." (Epilogue p. 358.)

Finally; we ground this article, as well as all other articles of our Faith, not on any man's *private interpretation* of Scripture, but on Scripture and Tradition, as expounded by the divine authority of the holy Catholick Church, which Chrift commanded all to hear and believe; faying to the Apoftles, when he fent them, and in them to their fucceffors, *He that believeth and is baptized, fhall be faved; and he that believeth not fhall be condemned.* (Mark xvi. 16.)

EXHORTATION. *Praife God in his Saints.* (Pfal. cl. 1.) Confider, that in honouring his faithful friends and fervants feated with him in eternal blifs, you honour him.

As the affair of falvation is our greateft concern, let us embrace all the helps the holy Church recommends to us: And as fhe has declared, *That the Saints now reigning with Chrift do offer their prayers to God for men; and that it is good and profitable to invoke them with humble fupplication, and to have recourfe to their prayers, aid and affiftance, for obtaining the benefits of God thro' his Son Jefus Chrift our Lord, who is only Redeemer and Saviour;* let us not be backward in imploring their interceffion now they are in heaven; we, who even confide in the prayers of one another on earth. It fhews great indifferency in our *unum neceffarium*, to flight fuch powerful means, by which, as we are well affured, God has given the moft extraordinary helps to others, fo as to work miracles in favour of thofe who confided in the Interceffion of his Saints: Of which, St. Ambrofe, St. Auguftin, and St. Chryfoftom among many others of the holy Fathers, may furely be admitted as good witneffes.

All

All antiquity confirms us in this belief. Great rafhnefs then it is to defpife that which fo great an authority recommends. (St. Aug. de Civ. D. l. 22.
c. 8.) (St. Ambrofe, ep. ad Sor.) (St. Chryfoſt.
de St. Bab.)

SECT. III.

On Devotion to the Bleſſed Virgin Mary.

From henceforth all generations ſhall call me bleſſed.
(Luke i. 48.)

Q. WHY do you pay fuch devotion to the Virgin Mary?

A. Becaufe fhe is the Mother of Jefus our Redeemer.

Q. Why do you give her fuch extraordinary honour?

A. For the fame reafon; becaufe fhe is *Mother
of God*, the greateft of the Saints; replenifh̓d with
grace above any other creature; for which *all generations ſhall call her bleſſed.*

Q. For what other reafon do you honour her?

A. She was honoured by God, Men, and Angels; are not thefe good reafons for us to honour
her?

Q. How was fhe honoured by God?

A. When he made choice of her to be the Mother of his Son Jefus.

Q. How by Angels?

A. When Gabriel the Archangel faluted her
with, *Hail Mary, full of Grace.*

Q. How by men?

Q. Firft by St. Elizabeth infpired by the Holy.
Ghoſt, crying out, *Bleſſed art thou among women,*
and

and bleſſed is the fruit of thy womb. (Luke i. 42.)
And ſince, *by all generations.*

2. Why does the Church call her *Mother of
God?*

A. Becauſe ſhe is the Mother of Chriſt, who is
true God, and true Man, and truly born of
her.

2. But don't you carry your devotion too high,
and think her more than a pure creature?

A. We think her *more pure* than any other creature, and bleſſed with higher *prerogatives* ; but ſtill
no more than a creature, made like others out of
nothing by the hand of the great Creator of all
things.

2. What authority have you for your devotion
to her?

A. The authority of the Church ; all Antiquity,
Tradition, holy Fathers, her own prophecy,
Henceforth all generations ſhall call me bleſſed, the
Salutation of the Angel Gabriel, and the Greet-
ing of Saint Elizabeth.

INSTRUCTION. We profeſs and believe,
that God is the ſole Creator of all things. The
pureſt and moſt excellent Creature is the work of
his hands, and originally ſprung from nothing but
his power : he alone then is worthy of divine
honour and worſhip. All the honour we give, and
devotion we pay to Saints and Angels, and to the
Virgin Mary, are refered to the great Creator of
all things, and redound to his honour ; otherwiſe,
we would not thus honour them. All the honours we give to them on account of their being beloved and honoured by him, are center'd in him.
We venerate thoſe moſt who are the neareſt to
him, and his moſt faithful ſervants ; and who are
neareſt to him, but the holy Angels, the Virgin
Mary,

Mary, and the Saints? This is the true belief of a Catholick.

It is true, we honour the Virgin Mary more, and have a greater veneration for her above all the Angels and Saints, for many fingular reafons. Firft; becaufe God elected her to be the Mother of our Redeemer, and by being the Mother of Jefus, fhe is become the Mother of God, as being truly the Mother of him who is both God and Man. Thus her dignity being above any other Saint, entitles her to greater veneration. Secondly; we have this fpecial veneration for her, becaufe God feems fo to command: *Henceforth all generations fhall call me blef-fed.* Thirdly; we honour her for her geat preroga-tive of fanctity above all other Saints; as, *full of grace, bleffed among women*; the moft bleffed of all women by the fruit of her womb. Is fhe not in thefe prerogatives greater than all Angels and Saints. We have therefore a fpecial veneration for her, becaufe fhe was honoured by God, Men, and Angels; God the Father honoured her, *when he regarded the humility of his handmaid*, and chofe her for the Mother of his Son. The Son honoured her, by taking flefh, and being born of her. The Holy Ghoft honoured her, when God the Son *was conceived in her by the Holy Ghoft.* 'Tis her fingular preroga-tive to be both Mother and Virgin: Never had Mother fuch a Son before; nor Son fuch a Mother. We honour her then with the Angel Gabriel, faying, *Hail Mary, full of grace, our Lord is with thee*: And with St. Elizabeth, when we fay, *Bleffed art thou among women, and bleffed is the fruit of thy womb, (Jefus)*: And with the Church, faying: *Holy Mary, Mother of God, pray for us finners, now, and in the hour of our death.*

Yet when we call her *Mother of God*, as was defined in the Third General Council at Ephefus

againft

againft Neftorius, we do not pretend that fhe is
the Mother of the Divinity; but by being Mother of him whom in the fame perfon is both God
and Man; hence, as fhe was by St. Elizabeth truly
called *Mother of her Lord*; fo now by the Church,
Mother of God. If you fay fome carry their devotion for the Virgin Mary too high; I know of
none well inftructed Catholicks that do fo. The
Catholick Church never approved, but ever reproved all fuch abufes. But tho' fome abufes fhould ftill
remain amongft ignorant people, muft all veneration
and refpect for the Mother of the world's Redeemer
be forgot and laid afide, as it feems to be amongft
our adverfaries?

As for miraculous Images of the Virgin Mary,
our Church has declared, *there is no virtue in them.*
'Tis not from the *Image*, but from the *Perfon* it re-
prefents, much good may be expected, as being in
fuch high favour with God; yet only from her,
as an *Interceffor* with God; from him, as the
giver of it. And if he has wrought fuch wonders by other Saints, fo furely he may do by her
powerful Interceffion, as he did at the Marriage of
Cana. (John ii. 11.) To fly to her Interceffion,
is in effect to fly to the Aid of her Son, of whom
fhe obtains all bleffings-for us: By honouring the
Mother we honour the Son, becaufe we honour
her on his account: We confefs with St. Epiphanius, that *Mary ought to be honoured, but God
alone adored.*

All Chriftian people and nations from the beginning of the Church, and all Antiquity, have
ever held her in high veneration. The Fathers in
their writings, the founders of religious Orders in
their Conftitutions, the Church in her Liturgies, all
feem in concert to have employed their tongues and
pens to exprefs their high veneration for her, and

to

to recommend the fame devotion to pofterity. How many Cathedrals, and other Churches throughout Chriftendom, are dedicated to God under her named; and, even in Proteftant Countries, ftill retain her name without fear of Idolatry? In this is fulfilled that faying; *From henceforth all generations fhall call me bleffed.* (Luke i. 48.)

To conclude; this is the faith of the Catholick church: That the Virgin Mary is a Creature as much as any other Creature, tho' *purer* than any other. That all the grace with which fhe was replenifhed on earth, was God's gift; and the glory fhe now poffeffes, his reward. That there is but One only God; Him alone to be adored and worfhipped with divine honour. Him alone to be prayed to as the giver of all good gifts. Him alone to be ferved and trufted in as God. He alone is the Creator of all things. All the Saints and Angels, and the bleffed Virgin Mary, are the work of his hands: And all the help we receive by their interceffion and our fupplications to them, proceeds from God: To whom be all honour and glory given for ever and ever. *Amen.*

EXHORTATION. Learn now, O Chriftian, from the Catholick Church, to honour the bleffed Virgin Mary the Mother of your Redeemer, fo highly honoured by God, men and angels. Honour her on account of her election to be the Mother of Chrift, *Mother of God.* This is the fource of all other her prerogatives: hence, unfpotted and without fin: hence, *full of grace*: hence, Mother and Virgin: hence, *by all generations bleffed.* O take her, as St. John did, recommended from the crofs, take her for your Mother: behold thy Mother; Mother of all Chriftians, help and refuge of all finners, under God. Fly then to her patronage in all your neceffities; beg her powerful interceffion for you to her Son Jefus: As fhe interceded at the marriage of Cana, and was heared; fo will fhe be a no lefs powerful advocate for you,

now

now she is reigning with her Son in glory. Say then with the Church, Holy-Mary Mother of God, pray for us sinners, now, and in the hour of our death. Amen.

SECT. IV.

On *some particular Devotions to the Virgin Mary.*

Behold, from henceforth all generations shall call me blessed. (Luke i. 48.)

Q. WHAT is the common address of the Church to the Virgin Mary?

A. Even that of the Angel Gabriel: *Hail Mary, full of grace*; from which is derived the *Rosary* and the *Angelus Domini*, much used in Catholick Countries.

Q. Why do Catholicks so often repeat the *Hail Mary?*

A. To commemorate the Incarnation of the Son of God; to honour his Mother, and to beg her intercession for us sinners.

Q. What is the meaning of the *Rosary*, or *Beads?*

A. 'Tis a devotion directed to obtain God's blessings, thro' the intercession of the Mother of God.

Q. But why so many times *Hail Mary* for once *Our Father?*

A. Because as often as we repeat the *Hail Mary*, we commemorate the Incarnation of the Son of God; hence the Rosary is so composed, as to commemorate all the mysteries of our Redemption.

Q. But is not this praying ten times more to the Virgin Mary than to God?

A. This is your mistake; every time we repeat the *Hail Mary*, we pray to God thro' her intercession. The same is to be said of all invocation of Saints;

we

we only beg of the Virgin Mary and the Saints to pray to God for us and with us.

Q. What is the *Angelus Domini?*

A. It is to put us in mind of our redemption : It is repeated three times in the day, morning, noon, and evening, that so great a benefit may never be forgot; and to accuftom us to pray often : *We fhould pray without ceafing.*

INSTRUCTION. All our addreffes, devotions and fupplications to the bleffed Virgin Mary, are done chiefly with refpect to her Son Jefus : All the veneration we have for her terminates in him, from whom all good is come both to her and to us. Thus, when we addrefs to her in the *Hail Mary*, 'tis to commemorate her Son's Incarnation, to honour alfo the Mother, and beg her interceffion for us: adding with the Church, *Holy Mary, Mother of God, pray for us finners, now, and in the hour of our death.*

As to the Rofary, 'tis a method of repeating the *Angelical Salutation*, with great benefit to the foul, by contemplating the chief myfteries of our Redemption, even from Chrift's conception to the coming of the Holy Ghoft; and concludes with commemorating the joys and glory of the bleffed Virgin Mary, and all the Saints. Now, can this be called Superftition ; or can he be a true good Chriftian, who deprives himfelf of every pious thing that infpires him with the thoughts of falvation ? For what can be a greater motive to a good life, than to be put in mind of what Chrift has done and fuffered for us, and the bleffings he hath beftowed upon us ? This is the very end of this devotion of the *Rofary.*

But is not our repeating the *Hail Mary* ten times for once *Our Father*, a difhonour to God ? fuch praying feems worfe than not praying at all : Does it not fhew, that we place a greater confidence in the Virgin Mary than in God ?

This

'This is our adverfaries miftake: When we fay, *Holy Mary, Mother of God, pray for us finners*; it is not true, that we pray to the Virgin Mary, and not to God: for as our Faith teaches; That *every good and perfect gift is from above, defcending from the Father of lights,* (Jam. i. 27.) and there is no Catholick but knows and believes this truth; accordingly all our prayers and petitions, whether we addrefs them to God ourfelves, or by fome Saint praying for us, they are ftill directed and made to him for the things we want, and in him we hope for the grant of them. When I beg the Virgin Mary to pray for me, is it not with a good hope that by means of her interceffion, God will hear me, and grant my petition? Is not my petition then properly made to him? Altho' therefore, I were to repeat the Hail Mary a thoufand times, it is not true that I pray more to her than to God; becaufe every time I beg of her to pray for me, I do in effect pray to God. Nor is this in any fenfe difhonouring God; for when we fay, *Holy Mary, pray for us*; we make her an humble fuppliant to God. And if we, who are finners, are thought to honour him and do an act of religion every time we call upon him in humble and devout prayer; much more do the Saints in heaven and the Virgin Mary honour him, when they fall down before his throne to pray for us and with us: What is this, but acknowledging that he is above them all, above the higheft in heaven, and that all good gifts are his? Can this be a difhonouring of God?

Neither is it true, that we place a greater confidence in the Virgin Mary than in God; but only that we confide more in her interceffion than our own prayers; knowing this truth, that *we often afk, but do not receive, becaufe we afk ill*; (Jam. iv. 3.) We therefore diftruft our own prayers, and have recourfe to the prayers of the Virgin Mary, and the

the Saints, which is an act of humility; 'tis alfo acting according to the orders of God, who will have finners have recourfe to the prayers of the juft, declaring to us, that *the conftant prayer of the iuft man prevaileth much*; (Jam. v. 16.) Hence, we read in Scripture, that God himfelf by a fpecial revelation, fent finners to the Saints to intercede for them, as he did Abimeleck, king of Geraris, to Abraham : *Now therefore*, fays God to him, *reftore to the man his wife, becaufe he is a Prophet, and fhall pray for thee, and thou fhalt live.* (Gen. xx. 7.) As alfo, he fent the friends of Job to him, that he might pray and offer facrifice for them to appeafe the divine wrath : *My fervant Job fhall pray for you; I will admit of his face, that the folly may not be imputed to you ; for neither have ye ftoken before me the things that are right.* (Job xlii. 8.) In like manner, we read how the Ifraelites in diftrefs, addreffed themfelves to Mofes and Samuel to avert the wrath of God from them. (Numb. xxi. 7. & 1 Kings vii. 8.)

What more decifive from the word of God, to authorife our practice of applying in our neceffities, to the interceffion of the Saints ? Yet it would be a ftupid error, and mere folly, to conclude from what God ordered thefe finners to do, that the Saints are more merciful than God. No : God, is infinite in mercy, and he is alfo juft; and the order of his juftice and providence requires, that the prayers of the *Juft* fhall prevail fooner with him than the prayers of finners ; at the fame time he fhews his mercy to finners by fparing them at the interceffion of the Juft. Let us not then be fuch proud Saints as to think we ftand in need of no other Saints to intercede for us.

The Rofary being thus vindicated, and proved to be an excellent devotion, it is recommended to all Chriftians, but is particularly ufeful to the un-

learned

learned who cannot read : And to others who
are diſabled for want of ſight or otherways from the
uſe of prayer-books; by the means of this devotion
they may be as conſtant in prayer, as thoſe who
have choice of books.

As to the *Angelus Domini* ; it is a ſhort devotion to
put Chriſtians in mind, even amidſt the tumults and
diſtractions of life, to give God thanks for the benefit of our redemption ; and is fixed at three times
of the day, morning, noon, and evening ; that we
may never forget the bleſſing of our Redeemer's
coming, but imprint him in our mind and memory ; and learn to pray to God inceſſantly : *We
ſhould pray at all times, and not fail herein.* (Luke
xviii. 1.)

EXHORTATION. O Chriſtian ! look upon
all the addreſſes which the Church makes to the
Virgin Mary, as made to her beloved Son thro'
her interceſſion. O raiſe up your heart and mind
to him every time you repeat this angelical Salutation, *Hail Mary !* and return thanks for the great
myſtery of your Redemption. And can you repeat
the memory of it too often, when ſuch bleſſings
have come therefrom ? O think of thoſe eternal
evils you once incurred by ſin ! Think of thoſe
eternal bleſſings you reaped by Chriſt's coming and
his divine grace : Once ſlaves of the devil, now
ſons of God : Infinite once was your miſery ; now
infinite is your glory ! And will you lay aſide and
forget this great bounty of Chriſt your Saviour, expreſſed in the angelical Salutation ; and ſlight ſo
powerful an Advocate to your bleſſed Jeſus as the
Virgin Mary ? who, as ſhe is the Mother of
Chriſt, ſhe is alſo the Mother of all Chriſtians :
*Holy Mary, Mother of God, pray for me, now, and
in the hour of my death. Amen.*

S E C T. V.

On Holy Pictures and Images.

To God alone be Honour and Glory for ever.
(Rom. xvi. ver. ult).

Q. WHAT is the intent of so many Pictures and Images in Churches?

A. They are as so many books to the ignorant, to put them in mind of Christ, and all the mysteries of our redemption; as also of the Virgin Mary and the Saints, that we may follow their example.

Q. But is there not danger of idolatry in setting so many pictures and images before the eyes of the ignorant people?

A. No: The faithful are so well instructed from their childhood in the belief of one only God, and of the meaning of holy Images, that idolatry, and all danger and shadow of it, is entirely vanished in all Catholick Countries.

Q. Is not your devotion and veneration of them carried to excess?

A. No: Strictly speaking, 'tis not the inanimate image we venerate, but the person it represents, whose memory is dear to us: Our veneration does not stop at the Image, but passes to the Prototype, the person or things represented by it.

Q. Do you think there is any virtue in holy Images?

A. No: There is no virtue in them: They neither see, nor hear, nor help us.

Q. What benefit then do you receive by them?

A. They movingly represent to us the mysteries of our redemption, and the acts and martyrdoms of the Saints.

Q. Is

Q. Is not the use of Images against the commandment, *Thou shalt not make to thyself any graven thing?*

A. No: They are not idols, or images of false
Gods, nor worshipped as such; which is the thing
forbid by that commandment.

INSTRUCTION. The faith of our Church
is best known from the decrees of her General
Conncils, where this article of the veneration of
holy Images is defined. First, in the Nicene Council, held An. Do. 787. against the hereticks of those
times, called *Iconoclasts*, or *image-breakers*, Calvin's pre-
decessors. This Oecumenical Synod defined as follows.
" The Images of Christ and his Saints are to be
" retained and placed in the Churches; that at the
" sight of them the memory and affections of the
" beholders may be excited towards those who are
" represented by them: And we are to salute and
" pay an honorary bowing down to the said Images,
" like as is given to the figure of the holy cross,
" to chalices, to the books of the gospels, or such
" like sacred utensils; but not *Latria*, which, as
" true faith teaches, is due only to God." (Act. 7)

The decree of the Council of Trent is worded to the
same purpose. " The Images of Christ, of the blessed
" Virgin Mother of God, and of other Saints, are to
" be kept and retained, especially in Churches, and
" due honour and veneration to be given them:
" not for any divinity or virtue which is believed
" to be in them, or that any thing is to be asked
" of them, or any confidence to be placed in them,
" as was anciently done by the heathens, who put
" their trust in idols, but because the honour which
" is done to the images is referred to the prototypes
" which they represent. So that by the Images
" which we kiss, and before which we kneel and
" uncover our heads, we adore Christ, and venerate
" the Saints, whose pictures they are; as the Coun-
" cils,

" cils, efpecially the fecond of Nice, have defined
" againft the impugners of images." (Coun. of
Trent, Seff. 25.)

Holy images therefore, are ufed in Churches for
feveral good ends; as well for ornament, as for inftruction of the ignorant; but chiefly, as helps to
devotion: While they movingly reprefent the myfteries of our redemption, and place before our eyes
the acts and martyrdoms of the faints, whofe example we profefs to follow. While my eye is on the
picture or image of Chrift, I have the imagination
of him in my mind; him I venerate, him I adore.
If I have a veneration for his image, it is becaufe
it is *his image*, and puts me in mind of him: The
veneration then which I have for the image, does
not ftop there, but is referred to the prototype, that
is reprefented by it. As all the Faithful are well
inftructed herein, and know there is *no virtue* or
divinity in holy images for which they are to be
adored; and that they neither fee, nor hear, nor
help us; there can be no danger of idolatry while
we kneel or pray before them.

There have been many miraculous well-attefted
cures wrought in the Churches, to reward the piety
of fuch as came to recommend their diftreffes to the
interceffions of the faints, and the Virgin Mary,
before their images: Yet thofe wonderful cures are
not to be attributed to any power or divinity in the
image; but to the almighty power of God, moved
to work thofe miracles, by the prayers of his faints,
to reward the faith and piety of thofe who confide
in his power; as alfo to atteft the faith of his
Church, and give a divine approbation of her religious practice of the invocation of faints, and veneration of holy images. However, we do not
pretend the hiftories of all thofe miraculous cures
are to be believed as articles of Faith; but only to

F. be

be credited as far as they appear certain. Hence, the Council of Trent decrees; *That no new miracles be admitted for true, 'till the bishop of the diocese has examined, and approved them.* (Seff. 25. de sacris imag.)

But what virtue, you say, in crosses or images to fright the devil; to diffolve charms; or drive away difeafes?

No Catholick pretends there is any fuch virtue in them : The Council of Trent exprefly defines that *no virtue or divinity refides in them.* Now, the decrees of General Councils are the rule of our faith and practice. When therefore, Catholicks fign themfelves with the fign of the Crofs, or fet up that fign in their Churches or houfes; they mean nothing more but to invoke God's Affiftance againft evil fpirits, and all that deal with them thro' Jefus Chrift crucified; which I conceive may put them to flight, and do all wonders for us.

That many fuch wonders have been done, very authentic hiftories teftify. This is owned by Doctor Covel, an eminent Proteftant writer of the Church of England, in his anfwer to Burges, (p. 138.) " No man can deny, fays he, but that God after " the death of his Son manifefted his power to the " amazement of the world in this contemptible " fign, as being the inftrument of many miracles."

But what means our adoration of the Crofs, efpecially according to the ceremony on Good Friday?

I anfwer; That 'tis not the graven image, but Chrift crucified reprefented thereby, is the object of our adoration that day: His image we venerate becaufe it is *his image,* and puts us in mind of the death he fuffered for us; but him only we adore with divine honour.

But is there not fomething more done to the Crofs, feeing in the hymn for that feftival we read thefe words :

words: *All hail O Cross our only hope :*
Increase the grace of the devout:
And blot the crimes of sinners out.

We answer, that the word Cross is here taken for Christ crucified, as it is twice over by St. Paul in one chapter, where he says; *Lest they may suffer persecution for the Cross of Christ.* And again; *God forbid that I should glory save in the Cross of our Lord Jesus Christ.* (Gal. vi. 12. & 14.) Was St. Paul an idolater for glorying in the *Cross* of Christ? What more common in Scripture, and other writers, than such metaphors? And what more easily understood? They are the elegancies of style, and no reader takes them to the letter, but according to their figurative meaning.

But after all; is not all veneration of images contrary to the commandment; *Thou shalt not make to thyself any graven thing, nor the likeness of any thing that is in heaven above, or in the earth beneath, or in the waters under the earth; thou shalt not bow down, nor worship them.*

Those who make this objection should reflect, that this commandment only forbids the making or worshipping of idols, or *images, of false Gods,* such as the heathens worshipped : So Moses himself explains this precept in the book of Exodus, where he repeats it again in other words; *Ye shall not make Gods of silver; neither shall you make unto ye Gods of gold.* (c. xx. 23) Now, when Catholicks make and venerate holy images according to the approved custom of the Church, they neither make golden Gods, nor silver Gods, nor wooden Gods; they neither make idols of them, nor give them *Latria,* or divine honour; for this is contrary to the sense and declaration of their own Church and General Councils.

To conclude; this is the doctrine of the holy Catholick Church: That a respect and reverence

is

is due to all such things as relate to the honour and service of God: To the book of the holy Scripture, as containing God's holy word: To Churches, as the house of God: To the Saints, as to his true servants: To altars and sacred vessels, as being consecrated to his service: To pictures and images of Christ, as renewing the memory of all the mysteries of our redemption: To'the images of the Virgin Mary, the Apostles, and other Saints, by whom he has converted the world, and wrought all wonders.

EXHORTATION. O Christian, see what helps God gives to encourage piety and devotion even by inanimate things; for what are images and pictures but inanimate figures? Yet what good may be drawn from the sight of them, tho' there is no virtue in them; they bring to our minds the most holy persons and things, and aid us even to penetrate into heaven. Can you lift up your eyes and behold a crucifix, and not think of the Author of life and salvation? Can you behold a picture or image of the blessed Virgin Mary, and not think of her that gave him birth? How can you behold the images of the Apostles, Martyrs, Confessors, and not think of those by whom God converted the world?

SECT. VI.

On the Veneration of sacred Relicks.

Praise ye our Lord in his Saints. (Psal. cl. 1.)

2. WHAT warrant have you for the veneration of the Saints Relicks?

A. The holy Scripure; antiquity; the ancient Fathers; the authority of the holy Catholick Church.

2. But

Q. But are not the Faithful in danger of venerating falſe Relicks for true?

A. No: T e Church takes all care by her Canons to prevent ſuch abuſes.

INSTRUCTION. Concerning the veneration of Relicks the Council of Trent has defined: " That the holy bodies of the Martyrs and other " Saints now living with Chriſt, which were once " living members of Chriſt, and templ·s of the " Holy Ghoſt, and which are by him to be raiſed " again to life, and to be glorified, are to be ve- " nerated by the Faithful; and that many benefits " are imparted to men thro' theſe Relicks: So " that thoſe who affirm there is no veneration or " honour due to the Saints Relicks, or that ſuch " their Relicks, and other monuments of them, " are in vain honoured by the Faithful, and viſited " in memory of them, in hopes of obtaining ſome " benefit thereby, are to be utterly condemned, as " the Church already has and does condemn them." (Seſſ. 25.)

Our profeſſion of Faith then, ſays; *That the Saints Relicks are to be venerated:* But how to be venerated? With ſuch veneration as is given to other ſacred things, as to the ſacred veſſels, to Altars, to Churches confecrated to the ſervice of God. We venerate the dead bodies, the bones, the duſt of thoſe holy perſons, as having been victims to God, by their mortifications and martyrdoms; ſanctified by his grace, and the living temples of the Holy Ghoſt: Knowing that theſe their Remains are preordained to a happy reſurrection and an eternal glory, and are allied to their ſouls now reigning in bliſs. Their memory ſhould never die, but ever live; and their ſepulchres and Relicks remain, to keep alive the memory of their good works and heroick virtues, which have made them

compa-

companions of Angels, and to excite mankind to imitate such great examples.

Our adversaries object, that at the best this is but a will-worship, which St. Paul condems as folly and superstition, in his epistle to the Colossians : (c. ii. v. 18.)

Now, I suppose by *will-worship* they mean that which has no authority from the word of God : Let us see then, whether the word of God does not give some sanction to this our devotion. It is written in the Acts of the Apostles, that *God wrought several miracles by the hands of Paùl, so that from his body were brought unto the sick, handkerchiefs and aprons, and diseases departed from them, and the evil spirits went out of them.* (c. xix. 11, 12.) Why may not Catholicks then, without superstition, apply the linen in which the bodies of the Martyrs have been wrapped to the sick? by which means many undoubted cures have been wrought.

In the fourth book of Kings we read: *And Eliseus died, and they buried him ; and the bands of the Moabites invaded the land at the coming of the year. And it came to pass, as they were burying a man, behold they spied a band of men, and they cast the man into the sepulchre of the Prophet Eliseus; and when the man was let down and touched the bones of Eliseus, he revived and stood upon his feet.* (c. xiii. 20, 21.) Here is another stupendous miracle wrought, even to the raising a dead man to life, only by touching the sepulchre and bones of the dead Prophet. Does not this authorise our veneration of the Saints Relicks and sepulchres, when we see such a miracle recorded in holy Writ, as done at the sepulchre of a Saint, even before the gates of Heaven were opened by Christ, and before the soul of the Saint was admitted to bliss?

In

In the earlieſt days of Chriſtianity great veneration was paid to the Relicks of the Saints and Martyrs. The ancient Fathers and Doctors of the
Church defended it; and none but hereticks and
infidels ever oppoſed and condemned it; ſuch as Ju-
lian the Apoſtate, Eunomius, Vigilantius, as may
be ſeen in the writings of St. Hierom and St. Auguſtin. St. Hierom in particular, attacked Vigilantius, who gave the Cathclicks of his time the appel-
lation of *duſt-worſhippers.* " Vigilantius, ſays he,
" fights with an unclean ſpirit againſt the Spirit of
" Chriſt, by aſſerting that the tombs of the Mar-
" tyrs are not to be venerated. The devils with
" whom Vigilantius is poſſeſſed, roar at the Relicks,
" and confeſs they cannot bear the preſence of the
" Martyrs." (con. Vigil.)

In a word; innumerable undoubted miracles have
been wrought, in favour of ſuch as came with Faith,
to viſit the tombs and Relicks of the Martyrs: An
ample relation hereof may be read in the epiſtle of
St. Ambroſe to his ſiſter, recounting the miracles
done at the tranſlation of the Relicks of St. Gerva-
ſius and Protaſius: And in the twenty-ſecond book
of the City of God, chapter the eighth, by St. Auguſtin of the prodigies done at the Relicks of St.
Stephen in Africa: And in St. Chryſoſtom, on
the tranſlation of the Relicks of St. Babylas, at
Antioch.

If you reply; There may be abuſes in taking falſe
for true Relicks; ſtill the doctrine of the Church is
true; *That the Relicks of the Saints are to be venerated.*
This is all ſhe teaches: and ſeeing ſhe lays no tye
upon the Faithful, of believing every pretended Re-
lick to be true; the members of the Church are
obliged to give no further credit to them, than as
far as they ſee them authenticated by the Prelates,
and have ſufficient grounds to merit their reſpect.

(Coun.

(Coun. Trent, Seff. 25.) As for falfe Relicks and miracles, the Catholick Church has taken all poffible care to detect and difcountenance them, and has ordered that they be ftrictly examined into by the Bifhop of every diocefe, before they are propofed to the veneration of the public. (Coun. Trent, Seff. 25, towards the end.) There may be falfe as well as true gofpels: Falfe as well as true Prophets: Falfe as well as true Preachers: Muft all be branded for impoftors becaufe fome are fo? And true Relicks be defpifed, becaufe fome are counterfeited? It is plain, that it is not the intention of thofe who govern the Church, to encourage the Faithful to the veneration of falfe Relicks: Join then with the Church, in the veneration of fuch as are of undoubted credit; and fhe preffes you no farther. Private abufes being all reproved, and ordered to be reformed by the Prelates in their feveral diftricts, cannot furnifh new reformers with fufficient grounds to abolifh a pious practice; recommended in the word of God, and by the univerfal tradition and authority of the primitive and prefent Church.

EXHORTATION. O Chriftian foul, pay a due veneration to all holy Relicks, as your pious anceftors have done before you. *Praife God in his Saints:* Let not their memory ever die: *The memory of the juft fhall remain for ever.* (Pfal. cxi. 7.)

Their facred remains are ftill allied, and hold an affinity to their fouls in glory; and will at the refurrection be re-united to them. Venerate them as you do all holy things that belong to God. Great wonders have been done in all times at the tombs of the Saints and Martyrs, which fufficiently atteft for our veneration of them. But ftill remember to imitate their holy lives, that you may become Saints with them, by the fame virtues which made them Saints.

SECT.

S E C T. VII.

On the Monuments of the Saints.

The memory of the Just shall remain for ever.
(Psal. cxi. 7.)

Q. WHAT is the end of erecting monuments to Saints and Martyrs?

A. To perpetuate the memory of holy men.

Q. What other intent have you in them?

A. To excite devotion, and to encourage ourselves and others to follow such great examples.

INSTRUCTION. The Scripture declares, that the memory of the just shall remain for ever: Is the wonder then great, if we erect rich and costly monuments to perpetuate their fame? But the Scripture again says, *The sinners memory shall rot.*

Now, if even worldly men raise such costly monuments to perpetuate the memory of sinners, (and have even intruded such monuments into places confecrated to God), men famed only for war, arts, or science; must the Church be condemned of superstition, for erecting monuments to holy men renowned for their heroic virtues and propagation of Christianity, and the working of miracles by the power of God? Who but an infidel, a Mahometan, a heathen, or a Calvin, can hold such sacred monuments in contempt?

Yet some who profess themselves Christians have acted still worse, in not only pillaging those sacred shrines, but even burnt the bodies and Relicks of the Saints, difperfing their afhes in the air and the waters, to the scandal of all Christendom. Even the sign of our redemption has been cast forth of the

Sanc-

Sanctuary. Well may be applied the prophecy of David to Calvin and his followers : *O God, the Gentiles have come into thine inheritance: They have polluted thy holy temple.--They have made the dead bodies of thy servants meat for the fowls of the air ; the flesh of thy Saints for the beasts of the earth. They have poured out as water their blood round Jerusalem, and there was none to bury them.* (Psal. lxxviii. 1, 2, & 3.)

EXHORTATION. Let Christians then look on the monuments of the Saints with a better eye than their adversaries do. Let not their memories ever die in your heart, as well for the great good they have done for the world, as for you. What! must we forget those holy Apostles, Martyrs, Doctors, to whom under God we owe our conversion and salvation? Must their memory perish who were so eminent in sanctity and all virtue, and have left so great an example for us to follow? No: Their monuments are ever sacred, as well as their memories are in benediction.---Away then with those pompous trophies of prophane heroes, and let them give way and due honour to those that are sacred in God. The memory of the one *will rot,* but the other *will remain for ever.* Give honour where God gives honour. *Thy friends, O God, are honoured exceedingly to me,* says the Psalmist. (Psal. cxxxviii. 17.) All sacred things ought to be held as sacred, as being the instruments of God's power to work wonders upon earth.

SECT. VIII.

On pious Pilgrimages.

The ground thou standest on is holy, put off thy shoes.
(Exod. iii. 5.)

Q. IS it not superstition to go on pilgrimage to visit the Relicks of the Saints, and holy places?

A. I cannot see the least room to censure such a pious practice.

INSTRUCTION. Even in the time of the Old Law, many came to visit the holy place in Jerusalem; and why must it now be deemed superstition to visit the holy land, the place of our redemption, and to trace with devotion the footsteps of our blessed Redeemer, who was born and suffered there? With like devotion many pious Christians have gone on pilgrimage to the shrines of the Apostles and Saints, where they knew many well-attested miracles have been wrought. And are not these journies of devotion to be preferred to those which many take to feed their curiosity and fancy, in travelling over mountains and vast tracts of country both by sea and land, to improve themselves in all vain and worldly knowledge? If the one is to make them fit for the world, the other is to make them fit for heaven.

EXHORTATION. Shall these pious journies then be cried down, which have no other end but to promote God's honour, and all sanctity and devotion? Alas! none but those, who want faith and religion, oppose them. Nothing torments some people more, than virtue flying in the face of vice.

As

As for you who profefs yourfelf God's fervant, praife and glorify him in all things that redound to his honour, and your own falvation. Honour thofe holy places in which he has been fo highly honoured. Go then, if not in body, at leaft in fpirit, to the holy land where your Redeemer was born, lived, and died. O venerate the ground he trod upon, and the print of his feet. Go alfo in fpirit to thofe holy places renowned for the Relicks of the Apoftles, Martyrs, and other Saints, the eftablifh- ers of our holy faith and religion. Their very duft is ftill facred, and will rife in glory. *Praife ye our Lord in his Saints.* (Pfal. cl. 1.)

C H A P. XIV.

On the Fafts of the Church.

Turn to me with all your hearts, in fafting, and weep- ing, and mourning. (Joel ii. 12.)

Q. ARE not your Church-fafts fuperfluous, and works of fupererrogation?
A. No: They are moft pleafing to God, and ben- eficial to our fouls.

Q. What warrant have you for this?
A. 'Tis a holy practice much recommended both in the Old and New Teftament.

Q. What is the end and intent of fo many fafts?
A. To punifh our fins paft: Fafting is a work of penance, it appeafes God, and prevents heavier judg- ments falling upon finners.

Q. But is it not fufficient to faft from fin.
A. Fafting caufes us to repent for fin, and is a means to make us more eafily overcome fin for the future.

Q. Did Chrift teach his followers to faft?
A. Yes: And fet the firft example himfelf, with leffons how to faft. (Matth. vi. 16.)   *Q.* But

Q. But doth he not say, *Not that which enters into the mouth defileth the man.* (Matth. xv. 11.)

A. 'Tis not the meat, which is eaten on a fast-day, defiles the soul; but the disobedience in eating forbidden meat.

Q. What are the conditions that make a perfect fast?

A. Carefully to avoid sin, and accompany your fast with true repentance, devout prayers and alms-deeds to the poor: This is the fast which God has chosen.

INSTRUCTION. Tho' the fasts of the Church are held by many as vain and superstitious, or at least superflous, and no ways necessary to salvation; they were always on the contrary held by antiquity as most acceptable to God, and most beneficial to the soul, and have, for time immemorial, been enjoined by the precept of the Church. This pious practice is so frequently recommended both in the Old and New Testament, and is so very necessary for doing penance for past sins, as also for overcoming vice, and leading us to virtue, *by chastising the body, and bringing it into subjection,* that it cannot but be accounted by a well-instructed Christian as a good and necessary religious work.

Fastings were in practice in the earliest times of Christianity: Nay, in those days more strict and frequent than in after-ages. St. Paul makes much mention of his *fastings* and *watchings:* (2 Cor. xi. 27.) The fast of Lent was instituted by the Apostles, as many of the holy Fathers do attest; and that it might be the more universally observed, it was enjoined as a precept to the whole Church by a decree of Pope Hyginus about the middle of the second century, as Eusebius in his Chronicle testifies.

Christ himself taught, that his disciples would fast when the bridegroom should be taken from them,

them, (Matth. ix. 15.) as indeed his difciples and Church have conftantly done unto this prefent day: He alfo gave them leffons how to faft, (Matth. vi. 16. & 17:) And fet the firft example by a forty days faft in the defart: Can it be fuperfluous or fuperftitious to follow Chrift's example, and to fulfil what he foretold of his followers?

The end of fafting is to do penance for our fins, that, as the *Ninivites* and other holy penitents did, we may find mercy at the hands of God. The intent of it alfo is, that we may, by bridling our appetites more eafily overcome fin, and be better difpofed to virtue and obedience to the Church, and learn to deny our own will. Can fafting then be deemed fuperftitious, when even God by his Prophet Joel calls upon his people, *to turn to him with all their. hearts in fafting, weeping, and mourning.* (Joel ii. 12.)

If you fay, the faft from fin *is the faft which God has chofen*; we alfo hold, that the moft rigorous faft is of no account with God, unlefs we refrain from fin; thefe muft go together to make a perfect faft: The Jews rendered their fafts difpleafing to God, whilft on thofe days they were found doing their own will, and oppreffing their neighbour, as God by his Prophet reproaches them: So the firft condition required to a good faft, is to renounce all fin, and to be converted to God with our whole heart, performing the faft in a fpirit of contrition and penance.

But is it not written, *That which goeth into the mouth doth not defile a man?* (Matth. xv. 11.)

We anfwer; 'Tis not the meat defiles the foul of a Chriftian, no more than fwine's flefh defiled the foul of a Jew: *For every creature of God is good,* (1 Tim. iv. 4.) But the thing that defiles the foul of a Chriftian, when he tranfgreffes the faft, is is the diſobedience of the heart in breaking the precept of the Church, which God has commanded all to hear and obey. Thus, our firſt parents were defiled in eating the forbidden fruit; not by the uncleanneſs of the food, but by their diſobedience in eating that which God had forbid them to eat.

EXHORTATION. Can you then refuſe to comply with this great duty of faſting, ſo acceptable to God, and beneficial to ſouls? Conſider the faſt of Moſes. (Deut. ix. 18) The faſt of the Iſraelites. (Judges xx. 26.) The faſt of Judith. (c. iv. 8.) The faſt of Eſther. (Eſther iv. 16.) The faſt of the Ninivites. (Jonas iii. 5.) The faſt of St. Paul, and the other Apoſtles and primitive Chriſtians. (Acts xiii. 3.) Let all theſe be conſidered with the happy effects that followed them, in removing the judgements of God which hung threatening over the heads of ſinners, and in drawing down his mercy on them; and then you will be convinced how great a good is faſting.

Nothing has been more ſtrongly recommended by all antiquity than faſting. The bleſſings that attend it, and the end propoſed by it, are well expreſſed by a holy Father and great Doctor of the Church, St. Chryſoſtom : " Faſt, ſays he, becauſe you have ſin- " ned: Faſt, that you may not ſin: Faſt, that you " may bring all bleſſings on yourſelf: Faſt, that you " may preſerve the grace of God in your ſoul."

The moſt perfect have need of faſting, to maintain their virtue: The moſt wicked, to ſue for mercy, and prevent God's judgments. Beware then of neglecting this eſſential duty.

Praiſe be to God.

INDEX.

FINIS.